Paul Dalla Rosa is a writer based in
have appeared in *Granta*, the *Pari*
Meanjin and *New York Tyrant*. In 2
was shortlisted for the *Sunday Times*
Exciting and Vivid Inner Life is his debut collection.

More praise:

'Pitch perfect, with undercurrents of sorrow and angst'
Kit de Waal

'Curious and unflinching ... deftly executed and cringingly
funny' *Guardian*

'These are bold, acerbic stories that draw out the surreality
of our disconnected, often brutal world' Seán Hewitt

'I love these voyeuristically addictive, funny and deceptively
simple stories. Paul Dalla Rosa has perfectly articulated
the bizarreness of human isolation and human behaviour'
Halle Butler

'A precise and perfect depiction of a particularly current
brand of emptiness and aloneness ... hilarious, brutal,
warm and tender' Abigail Ulman, author of *Hot Little
Hands*

'The contemporary urgency of his stories is intoxicating ...
This is such an exciting collection – writing this good is
thrilling, exhilarating' Christos Tsiolkas, author of *The Slap*

'Hilarious and heartbreaking ... It's deliciously deadpan,
often absurd, and painfully alive' Alice Ash, author of
Paradise Block

AN EXCITING

AND

VIVID

INNER LIFE

AN EXCITING

AND

VIVID

INNER LIFE

STORIES

PAUL DALLA ROSA

This paperback edition first published in 2023

First published in Great Britain in 2022 by
Serpent's Tail
an imprint of Profile Books Ltd
29 Cloth Fair
London
EC1A 7JQ
www.serpentstail.com

First published in Australia in 2022 by Allen & Unwin

'The Hard Thing' was originally published in *New York Tyrant* (2018);
'The Fame' was originally published in *Meanjin Quarterly* [Vol. 77 #1, 2018];
'COMME' was originally published in *Granta* (#144, 2018); 'An MFA Story'
was originally published in *Electric Literature* (Recommended Reading #434,
2020); 'Short Stack' was originally published in *McSweeney's Quarterly Concern*
(#62, 2020); 'In Bright Light' was originally published in *Granta* (#154, 2021);
and 'I Feel It' was originally published in *The Paris Review* (#239, 2022).

1 3 5 7 9 10 8 6 4 2

Printed and bound in Great Britain by
CPI Group (UK) Ltd, Croydon CR0 4YY

A CIP catalogue record for this book is available from the British Library.

ISBN 978 1 80081 013 6
eISBN 978 1 78283 969 9

For Stephen

Contents

The Hard Thing

I was living in Dubai and I didn't have a phone, a laptop either. I believed such things could betray me, or at least enable me to better betray myself. My father would call me on Skype but the calls would ring out. He sent emails I read later at work. They were generally the same. 'Answer my calls,' he'd write, and then he'd ask about my ex-boyfriend. He would list my ex's good qualities: that he remembered people's birthdays, that he was okay with my limited job prospects, that he routinely exercised. 'Most men are not like this,' he would say.

My father would also tell me about my future. He texted my birthdate and his credit card details to a psychic hotline that did readings on late-night television.

Today, my father wrote, 'It isn't great.' The stars indicated I was under the influence of an inverted Mars, which meant I could act like a body possessed. Unless I reconciled with certain energies, I would only ever know too late when I was truly loved.

'I think this is it,' my father wrote. 'I really do.'

I didn't find this as impressive as he did. To me, it read like an aphorism—it described most people.

The city was not what I'd anticipated. The air was either thick with sand or heavy with smog. When I first arrived I'd stayed in a serviced apartment I had rented due to misleading photos online. There were two small rooms and no windows. I could never tell if the sun had set. This was during Ramadan, so no one could serve drinks until it had. Every night I'd call the front desk and ask them: is it time, is it time?

I moved, but it didn't do much good. My new apartment, on the thirtieth floor of a complex that was built next to a series of man-made lakes, crawled with cockroaches. It had a kitchen, a communal bathroom, and a shared balcony the size of a shower stall. My room fit a single-size mattress and little else. Six people lived in the apartment. It's difficult to understand how.

I had come to make money and become someone else. I did make money; I paid no income tax, but my rent was expensive, outrageous, so I had little after spending on essentials. The company I worked for dealt in mineral rights. I used the company Amex card to book foreign nationals hotel rooms and to stock office supplies. I sent out priority mail and poorly proofread correspondence. Often all I would do for a day was stick little red stickers on contracts next to where clients had to sign. The documents were lengthy, in both Arabic and English, sometimes French, Mandarin. Like most things, I didn't need to understand them—I just had to avoid asking questions, had to get into a rhythm.

I'd sit there between glass partitions, drinking ice water, my eyes out of focus, my headache slowly dulling, and in this way feel at peace.

I was purifying myself, I thought, and so I rarely ate. When I wasn't working I went to the building's exercise centre and ran on a treadmill that wobbled and shuddered. I did squats on my balcony, and smoked cigarettes, looking out over Sheikh Zayed Road. I felt the heat. Most nights I descended the thirty flights and crossed the road to drink vodka and fruit juice in a hotel bar. Sometimes I would do small inexplicable things like smash a glass on the floor or take a late bus out to the dunes and scream. But I remained celibate. I was living where laws were meant to be moral. Sodomy was illegal, and so I figured my relationships could only be platonic. That was my idea: to exist as an ideal.

After seven months I met a friend for drinks. He was the only person I knew in the city from my life outside of it. He was the kind of friend you occasionally email but often lie to. I told him I had been here for less time than I had. Our drinks were arranged quickly. Maybe it was a date. I wanted to see if I could be a new person.

My friend was tanned and wore white linen. He looked ridiculous. He taught schoolchildren at an international school where he said the kids all spoke like movie stars. He told me that his students' parents often gave him gifts, either to influence grades or use local etiquette. He didn't know what to do with them. He was concerned about the ethics of it all. That's what he said: the ethics. He took a box out of his backpack and gave it to me.

'Take it,' he said. 'I've already been given five.'

It was a smartphone. I put it on the table. I stared at it while he continued talking. I didn't want to take it, but I didn't want to give it back either.

He told me that a twelve-year-old had come to class that week missing three fingers. I gasped. I was already drunk.

'Did he steal?'

'No, it was his birthday party the weekend before. His parents gave him a quad bike.'

My friend and I were different in many ways. He actually knew Arabs.

I said, 'That sucks.'

'They were going to reattach his fingers,' he said. 'But they couldn't because they were lost in the sand. The kids all thought it was kind of cool, though. But it's awful. You don't give a child something like that.'

My friend kept speaking and I was glad. The last thing I wanted was to talk about myself. I placed one hand on the smartphone's box, still on the table, then the other.

As he spoke I felt further and further away. I was reminded of when I saw a therapist. I saw her for two sessions. She had me write my problems on cue cards. We were to start on something easy. For a week she had me think about why I found it difficult to maintain personal relationships. I arrived at the next session and told her that I'd had a breakthrough—I just didn't want to have friends at all. The therapist pursed her lips and said, 'You're making this difficult.'

I realised neither of us was talking. My friend looked at me expectantly. I wasn't sure if he'd asked a question.

'I'd better go soon,' he said. 'Stephen is cooking tacos.

You can come if you want. Give your partner a call and have him come round too.'

'Go,' I said. 'I'm going to head home. We have our own tacos. I'll be out after I use the bathroom.'

I didn't go anywhere.

Close to ten, I watched a group of Emiratis come in, wearing white robes and headscarves. The bartender looked at them and shook his head. They shuffled out and came back half an hour later in Levi's. They drank martinis. I did too.

At close, I stumbled to a taxi stand. When we pulled up at my apartment building I felt wretched and alone. I got out of the car and the driver called out to me, 'Sir, please take your shoes.' I picked them up off the back seat and nodded demurely.

All in all, I thought the night went well.

In my room I plugged the new smartphone in and watched a red bar silently blink across the screen.

In the morning I crawled across my bedroom floor. I'd woken up there, tried to move towards my bed then let my head rest. I listened to hear if I could sense my flatmates. All was quiet. I stretched, then rolled over and saw a cockroach. We regarded each other for a moment, then it moved on.

I got up and walked to the balcony. I did what most people do: I took a photo of what I saw and put it online.

After our breakup, and sometimes before, using an app, I sent photos of my penis to men I hadn't yet met. Times were arranged. My ex knew nothing.

Naked with two other men, one of them said to me, 'Doesn't my boyfriend have a hot cock?' and I said, 'Yes,' as it bobbed in front of me like a cartoon character, kind of nudging my face. The boyfriend, on his hands and knees, breathed into my neck and repeated, 'Hot cock, hot cock, hot cock.'

A petite Asian student asked me to pee on him. The windows of his studio apartment were lined with aluminium foil. I drank a large glass of water and he kneeled in the shower.

I did other things, unsafe things, that didn't make sense at the time and make even less now. I clicked 'attending' on an invite to a sauna party, then I went and walked around in a towel. The towel came off and I had sex with a man, then another, and another, all raw. The last slicked his fist with Crisco. He hesitated. I told him, 'Put it in.'

The next day I went to the hospital and recounted my sexual history. The nurse in triage ticked a box: 'Exposure risk high.'

My ex and I were still together in the morning, then we weren't.

Afterwards, for thirty days and nights I had to swallow two pills that made my stomach churn, until slowly I didn't have to take them or worry about that one specific thing anymore, just everything else. I sent my ex messages telling him I loved him. I also sent him messages describing the men I had slept with, and photos of myself reflected in my bedroom mirror, naked, in the position of an animal, the position of a dog.

———

At work there was talk of a sandstorm, and then there was a sandstorm. The outside turned dark, a great and empty haze. It was still hot. I couldn't regulate my temperature. I shivered at my desk. I sweated. I looked at the papers in front of me and realised I didn't know what I was doing. There were rules, but I couldn't remember if I had them the right way round, whether a section had to be signed or if a signature there would make the contract invalid.

The director, an Italian man with an almost impenetrable accent, stopped at my desk and spoke to me. I thought he was speaking to me in Italian, and I didn't understand why he thought I could speak Italian. But he wasn't. He was just asking if I felt okay. I said, 'Si,' and then excused myself.

In the bathroom I sat on the toilet and set up my email account on my phone. There was an email from my father, the subject line, 'Last Night's Reading'. The body text just said, 'Do the hard thing.' I replied, 'What's the hard thing?' Then I looked at my junk mail and scrolled through an Abercrombie & Fitch advert. I rolled my shirt up and sort of pawed at myself, looking at the models.

That night I was in a hotel further down Sheikh Zayed Road. It was a kind of sky lounge, with neon lights and floor-to-ceiling windows that looked out onto the waters of the gulf, islands under their own construction, cranes in the sky. There were some businessmen in boat shoes. A woman in a floral dress read a travel guide.

I tried to read but it was hard. I had to be calm, which meant I had to be drunk. I had only brought a few novels with me into the country and so I reread the same ones. Instead of reading a whole book, I would read from the parts when the protagonist was at their lowest and in the last thirty pages somehow steps out of the narrative reborn.

I looked at my phone. I looked back at the book I wasn't quite reading then ordered another vodka soda. The woman sitting at the bar smiled at me.

I reread a few pages. In the novel a character travels to Sri Lanka and meditates with Buddhist monks. At one stage she walks onto a rocky beach, kneels, picks up two rocks and gouges her chest with them, then her feet, then her arms. Bleeding, she goes back to the monastery where no one says a word, partly because they do not speak. Eventually, with a shaved head, she gets on a plane for home.

I wondered if I had misjudged my plans, all of them, and then my phone vibrated on the table. It was an email. It was from my ex.

'I saw you're in Dubai. That's cool. I'm going to Europe but have a layover for two nights. Tips?'

I immediately replied.

I sat in the bar, then sent another email telling him to disregard the first email in which I said we should see each other, and then a third to disregard the second. There was a fourth but that didn't really say anything one way or the other. I put my phone down on the table, picked my book up, put my book down, picked my book up again and held it close to my face.

Someone touched my arm. I recoiled. It was the woman in the flower dress. She said, 'I love that book. There was a time when it was everything to me.'

I shrugged her hand off and got up.

'Sorry,' she said. 'I just really love that book.'

I said, 'You should work on having more dignity,' and walked away.

In my room I looked at my phone, and then, its screen glowing, slowly pushed it beneath my mattress.

For four days I stalked my ex's Facebook profile, dry-cleaned my shirts, listened to meditation audiobooks, stalked his Facebook profile, did push-ups in the dark of my room, sent off contracts at work, and stalked his Facebook profile some more.

On the fifth day I saw he checked in to the airport. He was boarding his plane. Here it was 1 a.m. on the morning of a work function and so nine hours later I was at the work function. It was brunch, which really meant hours of daytime drinking and a buffet. Using the company Amex card, which now rested in my shirt's front pocket, I had booked the function a month ago in a large hotel on The Palm, a man-made archipelago built for actors and business tycoons.

From where we sat on a deck I could watch the water, glittering through my sunglasses, and a helicopter pad, helicopters descending and ascending, men in white pants stepping in or out. Everyone was drinking guava mojitos, mai tais. For some reason there was also a magician. He just walked around doing tricks. Everyone from the office kept asking me, What's up with the magician?

I wasn't drinking. I ordered tonic waters with wedges of lime. It was refreshing. I thought, yes, this is what people do.

I sipped my drink then excused myself. I went to the bathroom. Everything was white marble. I entered a stall. I didn't know what flight he was on, so all morning I kept checking them all. I watched little glyphs of planes inch across a globe. My battery was running low. I came out of the bathroom.

'Can I charge my phone?' I asked the attendant. He didn't ask any questions, just nodded seriously and took it away. It was that kind of hotel.

I came back to the bar. I ordered another tonic water with a wedge of lime. I sipped it then asked for a small amount of gin. The bartender poured in a shot glass. I looked away. Then I said, 'Keep it going.'

I stood with our party. Everyone was drunk. Everyone was an expat. A woman kept telling the same story about a client who had taken her out for a lunch to discuss business matters. They'd sat on a deck, not unlike this one, but in a corner, at a small table. At one point she'd looked down and his penis was out of his pants. It was flaccid, she said, like a sleeping mouse. He'd smiled at her, zipped up his fly and left.

I told her that I loved her, and everybody laughed. I was optimistic. I was feeling good things.

I asked a waitress for my phone. It came back to me different. I didn't think it was mine and then I realised someone had just cleaned the grease off the screen. I hit the home button. My ex had replied.

I opened the email. It was one line: 'I don't think that's a good idea.'

———

The sun went down. People left. I kept moving deeper and deeper into the hotel. It was like a palace in a children's story: each door led to an even larger room. Except it was different because they were all bars. I asked a bellboy to take me to the darkest, most expensive one. I had been drinking for seven hours. Sunlight and gin and something else streaked through my veins.

I looked at each man I passed. I looked at their face, then their crotch. I scrutinised the bellboy. I wanted to swallow a thousand dicks, ten thousand dicks.

I sat on a stool and waved the Amex card to the bartender. I ordered three peach Bellinis and lined them up on the bar. I drank them quickly and made eye contact with strangers.

We drank shots of Patrón. I used the company credit account. I slid the card over the bar and started a tab. We had more shots.

'You're in the navy?' I asked.

'Yeah.'

'The Navy navy?'

'That's what I said.'

We were in a kind of booth thing. Our knees were touching—they didn't need to be. He was built, broad-shouldered, and had good skin and teeth. He reminded me of a horse and sounded like a porn star. Wholesome, American.

I said, 'How about we go to the bathroom and I suck you off?'

'What?'

'I said I have to go to the bathroom.'

I went to the bar and came back with drinks.

'There's a club we can go to,' he said. 'It's underground but cool. Safe.'

I didn't want to go to a dark club filled with other gay people, so I said, 'I don't want to go to a club filled with other gay people. We can stay here a while.'

He said he wasn't gay and I said whatever.

I finished my drink then drank from his. My knee was really pressed into his. I leant into him.

He got up to buy another round. I told him to put it on the tab.

I watched him walk to the bar. I watched him walk back.

I said, 'You have huge shoes.' I asked him to take one off. 'I want to see how big it is.'

I slunk down. The bar was very dark but also lit in that way bars are—you could see everything. I slid beneath the table. I tried to take one of his shoes off but it wouldn't come off. I was on my hands and knees.

'What the fuck are you doing?' His leg kind of pushed me, hard.

'I just want to put it in my mouth.' I bent my face down. I licked the shoe. I don't know how he knew when I was licking it as I was licking it but he kicked me right then. My vision turned white. A glass fell off the table but didn't break. I thought this was funny.

A man in a vest brought my card over and told me that maybe I should check in to my room.

I told him I wasn't sleeping at this hotel. I used the word establishment.

'Then you should leave.'

The navy man was already walking away. A security guard appeared and put a hand on my shoulder.

I said, 'You are not my judges,' and was taken to a taxi.

In the taxi I vomited, first on myself and then onto the backseat window. The driver started yelling. I repeated, 'I'm fine, I'm fine.' I vomited again. He yelled. I yelled. We both yelled. He said he was driving to the police station, that they would deal with me. I screamed, I howled. He said he wanted two thousand American. I blacked out.

I woke up on my bed, fully dressed, my clothes covered in bile.

The Amex card was gone. I checked my pockets, then I let the fact settle. It was just gone. I lay there, taking it in, then my thigh began to tremble at regular and insistent intervals. I pulled my phone from my pocket.

'Hello,' a voice said. 'Hello,' it repeated. It was my father.

'Hi,' I said.

'You answered.'

'I did.'

I stood up, took my clothes off, and, naked, holding the phone against my ear, walked slowly through the apartment and squatted on the balcony.

My father was speaking. There had been a reading. He was describing a card, a tarot card. A man was on a horse. He held a stick or something like a stick. I took deep breaths. I looked down at the lakes through the balcony's smudged glass. There was some kind of complication, my father said.

If the man is flipped one way it means a journey, a destination. If it's flipped the other, a false start, stasis.

'Are you listening?'

'Well,' I said. 'Which one is it?'

My father turned quiet. Then I heard his voice, soft and frail.

'It's hard to say.'

Comme

The Melbourne store was in an alleyway. There was nothing else in the alleyway, only red bricks and the store. We had no signage, though people persistently stood in front of the entrance and took photos of themselves. Sometimes they would do this inside. In these situations my staff were often unsure how to act. I told them to do what we always did: stand and wait for customers.

We played no music. Clothes hung from metal scaffolding. In shifts, time dilated. When customers appeared, they moved or seemed to move faster within the store than they did outside of it. I trained my staff to act indifferently towards them and pour cucumber water, at their discretion, to potential high-end clientele. These were mainly rich men and women from Beijing, Shanghai, or Asian teenagers using Amex Platinum cards.

When the store was empty—it was almost always empty—I would use a hand-held steamer to steam items before rehanging them, or I would track sales on a tablet. In all things I would aim to be an example by being very still, almost meditative. More than anything, I explained to new employees, the store was meant to be like a static image, a photograph in a magazine, dynamic only through shifts of light, the bold cuts of hemlines, a shirt's silhouette.

It was like this, the store vacant, me standing over the tablet, when the email came. It was brief and from our Asia-Pacific head of sales, a severe woman named Janelle who was based in Japan and with whom I sometimes had video conferences. She said that R, the founder of our label, would be coming. R would be in the country in two weeks' time on personal matters, but would, potentially, visit the store. 'You understand the gravity of this.'

I read the email three times. One after another, after another.

R was known for being reclusive. In the early eighties she had arrived at Paris Fashion Week with a staff of four. What she did there shocked people. Models walked in black upon black, distressed fabric, asymmetric cuts. Now she employed more than five hundred and had retrospectives at the Pompidou, the Met. A fellow Japanese woman, a fan, had once attempted to throw acid on her. Fashion bloggers at the time wrote that this was in fact an act of outsized love. I didn't have the same feelings towards her, but I understood how others might.

I was uneasy with most forms of devotion. When a Silicon Valley billionaire died, a man I was seeing went out and bought flowers and left them outside one of the billionaire's stores. He described it to me. The store glowed in the night and people stood in front of it in heavy jackets and cried. In response I said cruel things—well, really one remark that was too cutting, and he said, We are no longer dating.

I was a professional and I was good at my job. I managed the store to the precise specifications I had been taught or that were sent through in emails from corporate. Often these emails weren't directives exactly but quotes from R, something closer to proverbs, ways of being. 'The fundamental human problem is that people are afraid of change,' or 'Fashion is living, it is about every moment being alive.' I didn't often feel alive, but I tailored my managerial style as best I could.

I was not afraid of change. I had worked in my position for many years, but I was in my thirties and wanted them to lead to something else. The label was young and I was approaching the point at which I wouldn't be. R's visit would be important to something I had stopped speaking about aloud. My career.

When I told my boyfriend, he didn't respond directly but sent a message describing a glacier and a black sand beach. 'It's black. Really, really black.'

He was in Iceland discovering himself. Those were his words. He had done so before on trips to Alaska, Taiwan, Morocco, a string of European cities. He only travelled alone. Because of the time difference we mainly spoke at night.

I was lying in his bed. I slept in his apartment while he was away because it was more luxurious than mine— there was a doorman—and I felt anonymous in the Korean store below his building where I bought items I would otherwise feel self-conscious to purchase together: diet tonic water, dry shampoo, a lone cucumber, Chinese slimming tea.

My boyfriend sent a photo, but he sent the raw .CR2 file. I texted, 'Lo-res, send lo-res,' and he talked about a sauna in Reykjavik where they didn't put chlorine in the water, so you had to shower before you entered, but you had to shower in an open space where an attendant watched to make sure you used soap.

My boyfriend's father was a Chinese artist and his mother an English translator and so he felt the pull to distinguish himself as something constant and painful. His godfather was Ai Weiwei. He brought it up whenever we met new people. I would hear, 'Ai Weiwei, Ai Weiwei.' It was like a mantra he uttered until he reached a certain age and didn't want people to make the comparison. Now he just said he was a visual artist. There was never much art. Mainly he stayed in his apartment taking near-nudes of himself and building his Instagram following. I wasn't connected to Ai Weiwei and I didn't have rich parents. I weighed less than sixty kilos, bought expensive clothes and wore them.

The photo still hadn't loaded. I messaged, 'I can't see it.' I switched my phone from wifi to mobile data.

He started describing it, the black pebbles, the grey sea.

I said, 'I can see it now,' even though I couldn't.

He said, 'It's sad you're not here. You had to stay for the designer.'

I texted, 'I only just found out about the designer.'

'I know. But you had to be there for it. It works out.'

I didn't feel like replying to that.

An hour later my phone vibrated. 'I think you should masturbate in my bed.'

Then again. 'Send a photo.'

In the morning I showered and carefully did my skin regime. A cleanser, followed by toner, then moisturiser. Sometimes I also used serum.

As I massaged in the moisturiser I felt something dense and tender on the left side of my jaw. It was small and felt like a trigger point, a knotted muscle. I was familiar with them. When I slept I ground my teeth. It was a problem, causing tension headaches and, what concerned me most, chipped enamel.

I fed a pod into my boyfriend's espresso machine, relaxed my face, dressed, drank my coffee then took the elevator down and walked to the store.

I unlocked the front door, then locked it once I was inside. I liked being there before we opened. At a specified angle I sprayed the label's signature scent, or rather a scent based on our signature scent—not for sale but produced for this alone— twice on the ground floor and twice again on the loft level. This was always the time I felt my thoughts were clearest.

I was conflicted whether to inform my staff about R's trip. I was concerned about the possibility that if R did come they would recognise her, and, without warning, act in a way that would embarrass me. Or, even worse, almost unthinkable, they could mistake her for a customer.

As I thought this my phone rang.

A staff member said he was sick. 'I have a breakout. It's really bad.'

'Have you tried concealer?'

'I've tried. I can't cover it. I can't cover it.'

My staff often shared their personal problems with me—breakups, health complications, UTIs—to explain why, at little notice, they could not come to work. I allowed them to do so, or rather I would just stand there and be relieved once they stopped speaking into the phone.

I said, 'Fine.' Even understaffed I could manage.

The day would be Heidi, Sara and me. Heidi was twenty-six and had strong features which made her not conventionally beautiful but something more interesting and strange. She had the kind of face that seemed to dramatically shift when looked at from different angles or in different light. This was the first thing I noticed when I interviewed her.

I knew that Heidi wanted to be the manager because she often said, 'I want to be the manager. It would suit my skill set.' I wanted to explain to her that my position was poorly paid—a salary as opposed to commissions. Some weeks my staff would earn more than I did. At the same time, I did not want to tell her this because I told no one this.

The day wasn't busy. At one point I watched Sara standing with a Japanese woman. Sara, like most of my staff, studied fashion and mistook working in retail for working in the industry. This was understandable—I had once thought the same thing. She held the customer's card in one hand and one of the tablets in the other. They stood there for a long time. She shook the tablet. I walked over. She turned to me. 'It's not working. The point-of-sale is down.'

The screen lit up with a green tick.

'Oh, it's working now.'

I felt a muted sense of panic, and though I didn't often take a lunch break I took one and went to an office supply store. I printed recent photographs of R at different events, and then a lone paparazzi shot, taken on a street in Paris, of her drinking from a takeaway coffee cup. I came back and stuck them, with a torn-out page from *Vogue*, on one of the back room's walls.

In the store's group messaging channel I explained the situation. I ended with: 'For the next two weeks no one is calling in sick to shifts. No one is coming in late. No one is coming in hungover. If you do, I will suspend your store discount. I will suspend everyone's store discount.'

That night my boyfriend sent me a video of a geyser. He had taken the footage using a high frame rate and then played it back at twenty-four frames per second, slow motion. The frame showed a small circular pool. Slowly, a large bubble expanded and expanded until it was a metre, two metres high. It shimmered for one drawn-out moment and then the surface tension was too great and it shot into the air. I watched it, then watched it again.

Lying in my boyfriend's bed I couldn't say that I liked my life or that it was not full of small disappointments.

I was pretty. I was tall and slim, had delicate features, long hands and feet. My body was the kind of body that things were designed for, and other gay men tended to project onto it their own resentments or desires.

When I was younger I had the problem of men falling in love with me. People would wait outside the store to speak to me or they would wait inside until I served them. Occasionally there would be large gestures of affection and control—plane tickets, hotel rooms, reservations at restaurants I could not afford but never had to pay for.

I still got attention. It hadn't waned, but the value had depreciated. If a customer asked me out for a drink or to their apartment and I said I was seeing someone, they would narrow their eyes and I could tell that they could tell I was over thirty, probably close to thirty-five.

I often felt that I had made poor choices, that I had failed to capitalise in some generalised yet hyper-specific way. I had once learned Mandarin by slowly and persistently attending classes. I'd wanted to be transferred to the label's new flagship store in Beijing. The transfer never happened, and over time I stopped speaking the language to my boyfriend and we stopped watching Chinese films. He didn't mind.

We lived in separate apartments. We went to restaurants and exhibitions together, took photos of each other in soft light and uploaded those photos online. Often, as we lay in bed, my boyfriend would show me other men's Instagram profiles and ask if I thought they were attractive. Sometimes this made me emotional in ways I found difficult to explain.

We had threesomes with these same men and filmed them. We were good-looking and people wanted to see themselves flattened onto a laptop's screen. Sometimes, during the act, my boyfriend would say desperate things aloud. What I mean is: he would describe his penis.

I watched a homeless man in front of the store. He wore an oversized coat and paced the alleyway, then looked through the glass and sort of leered at us or at his reflection. No one would go out to talk to him. At one stage he kept bending down and hopping back up like he was doing squats or jumping jacks. This all occurred over several hours.

I let others tend to customers while I went to the loft level and pretended I was doing stocktake. Really I browsed eBay listings on one of the tablets.

There was a married couple who ran an online store with rare stock from our label. They found pieces from old runway shows, acquired them, modelled them themselves in strange places—car parks, fast-food outlets—then put the photos online and took bids. They were based in Japan and were profiled in online magazines. The prices were what you'd imagine: obscene.

I kept looking at a piece. It was a black padded shirt from the nineties, with bulges that distended the silhouette. High fashion but not too high fashion. It felt *now*.

Because I spent a large amount of time convincing people to buy clothing they would never actually wear, it was easy to convince myself the same. I imagined how I would look in the shirt and I imagined R walking in and appraising my outfit, my style, my store. Internally, in Japanese, she'd think, Yes, that is someone who knows what's going on.

This seemed worth the four thousand dollars they were asking. I made a bid.

Sara called out to me.

I came down the stairs. The store was empty and the homeless man was in front of the store window facing us. His dick was out. He was urinating onto the window and staring intently at Sara.

When he noticed me, he did—I don't know how to say it—a kind of flourish with the stream. It seemed effeminate. We stood there until he finished and shuffled away.

I called our cleaning company. They arrived hours after they said they would and used a high-pressure hose on the glass. Heidi sent me a message. 'Sara texted what happened. You should let her go home.' I resented this.

I let Sara go, and spritzed the store with room spray. Then I walked around and spritzed it again. I put a finger onto the tender spot on my jaw and pushed it.

I returned to the tablet. I tracked the store's sales figures, then I opened a new tab, looked at the shirt again, became nervous that someone might outbid me and so pre-emptively made a higher offer.

I had the package couriered express international. I had it delivered to the store, which was unprofessional, but I knew someone would be able to sign for it. It arrived within three days. The package lay in the back room next to the rack that hung the Spring line we would only wheel out, after hours, for important customers.

I had a video conference with Janelle. She was in Singapore. She always took the calls in different cities with different backdrops, like a news correspondent. Every year we had at least one exchange which involved me asking her to rethink my position while she stared off-webcam before saying she was thinking, and then stating implicitly, often explicitly, that many people wanted my role.

We spoke about numbers. We spoke about the numbers Janelle wanted to be seeing and I explained the numbers she was seeing. I told her the reactions we'd been having to the Spring line. Janelle nodded.

She asked about R's visit, and if the store was ready for it. I said, 'Immaculate.'

She said, 'Heidi said you have a photo-wall up.'

I said, 'How are you talking to Heidi?'

'Take the photos down. It's embarrassing. I need you to be across this. I need to know you can do it.'

'I can do it.'

'Good. That's what I want to hear.' She ended the call like in a movie. She never said goodbye.

I took the photos down, opened my jaw and closed it a few times, then stood on the shop floor. Heidi was with a customer. The woman kept pointing at a dress with a missing square of fabric in the front and Heidi was repeating that it wasn't cut out but 'deconstructed'. She repeated this monotone.

I wanted to kill myself but in the way that wouldn't actually kill me.

A man walked in. He was maybe in his fifties, but well put together, silvered hair. He was wearing a suit and sneakers. I recognised the sneakers. They were made of white Italian leather and retailed for nine hundred dollars. I figured he was an architect.

He stood next to the concrete plinth we kept our fragrances on. He looked at the different bottles. Heidi slowly oriented herself towards him, but she had to stay with her customer even though she knew it wouldn't be a sale.

I asked him how could I help. He said he wanted something 'fresh'. The man had a British accent. I nodded.

I spoke about the scents, listing their profiles, holding each bottle before I sprayed one spray on a white stick of paper and handed it to him. He asked difficult questions. After I said, 'notes of oxygen, pollution,' he said, 'But what does that mean?' When he was holding seven samples I asked if there was one he wanted to try.

He pointed to a bottle. It wasn't a signature scent but one in a series of concept lines. I sprayed his wrist and told him to let it settle, let it open on his skin.

The man smelt his wrist and nodded. He placed his arm back down by his side.

We stood there quietly.

He asked me to smell him. 'I want a second opinion.' He didn't raise his arm though, just sort of rotated it so that his wrist was exposed, crotch level. He waited.

I bent down to smell it. I said what I would've said about any fragrance on any customer.

'It's really deepened.' I looked up at him. 'That's the one.'

I sold him a 100ml bottle of perfume, two pairs of trousers and a sweater. It rang up to $3784. The man left me the name of his hotel and his room number. Later, I sent a long message to my boyfriend describing the whole thing. Not because I was considering going there but because I wanted attention. He replied instantly, 'Weird.' Then, 'I wonder if he would have paid you.' Then, a string of three cash emojis.

I laid the package on my boyfriend's bed and carefully slit the shipping tape. There was cardboard and layers of black tissue paper and then the shirt. Standing there I already knew it was a bad decision.

I put it on and looked at my reflection in the bathroom mirror. My first thought was that I had put it on wrong—this sometimes happened with customers in the store—but I hadn't. It was bad. The padding made me think of Lisa Simpson in the episode where she dresses up as the state of Florida. It looked like I was wearing a futon. I took a photo then googled 'Lisa Simpson Florida'. The resemblance didn't make me feel any better.

I sent an email saying I wanted to return it. The couple wrote back, immediately and politely, that they did not do refunds. They signed off together. I asked if I could do an exchange, then I lay in the shirt and looked at my face using my phone's camera. Where the sore spot on my jaw was sat a slightly raised mound. I fell asleep with my phone in my hands.

At 3 a.m. it vibrated. The couple had replied with a long, complicated message in Japanese I was almost certain meant no. I squinted and used Google Translate. It meant no.

I did what I felt I had to do in the situation. I went back to their site and made a separate offer on a 1996 see-through PVC vest.

The vest arrived and it was beautiful. To make myself comfortable in it I wore it naked around my boyfriend's apartment. I planned to pair it with the Spring collection's oversized striped poplin shirt. I was into it. I wore it and thought of an elegant hand, R's hand, picking me up and placing me somewhere else.

The night she arrived in the country I stayed back at the store. A shipment had come in but the stock hadn't synced with our system. I had to code each piece through manually and then put them back into their boxes and stack them. I wanted this done before R visited. I wanted things to be efficient.

I asked people to stay back. Everyone said no. As I closed, Heidi and Sara stood in the back room fixing their make-up. I got the sense that they were meeting other staff. Well, I overheard their conversation. A different label was having a party. It was an American label specialising in American streetwear but how American streetwear is worn in Asia. There would be photographers. I said to no one in particular, 'But it's a Wednesday night.'

The two of them giggled. I realised they were drinking. We kept very expensive champagne in a mini fridge in the back room for certain high-profile customers.

I didn't want to make a thing of it. I used to be like this. Fun. But I didn't want them to think Heidi had authority or that I wasn't the boss. I told them to go to the party and leave the bottle. It was half-full. I said I expected more from them. Then I got self-conscious and thought that was a stupid thing to say.

I stood on the empty shop floor and looked at the galvanised steel, the polished concrete, the clothes. It was dark outside and darker still in the store. I thought I should toast my future success, so I did. I drank champagne from the bottle then went to the back room and continued counting.

At one point I just sat in front of the back room's mirror and picked at my face. I thought, She's in the country, she's in the country. I saw myself in an airport transit lounge, business class, making conference calls, video calls. I imagined myself looking off-camera then telling someone my valued opinion.

I sipped French champagne. I was drunk. Tokyo Fashion Week, Paris. I imagined being given all the things I deserved.

I was smiling. I looked at my reflection and saw the mound on my jaw was bigger. It was a pimple, cystic and rising from deep beneath the surface. Red and inflamed, it protruded from my jaw. It was obvious when I stood in profile and even worse head-on. I inhaled and exhaled.

The Korean market beneath my boyfriend's building was open late. It sold skin products that were both harsher and in some instances more effective than what I regularly used. They didn't fuck around with natural ingredients like yuzu or neroli blossoms. They were chemical, all about results.

I asked the attendant for the strongest product they had. She handed me a foil packet that didn't really look any different from the others. It showed a smiling Korean woman. They all showed smiling Korean women.

'This is the strongest?'

The woman nodded.

I pointed at my face.

She whispered, 'Chemical peel.'

Back in my boyfriend's apartment, I cut cucumber slices and opened the foil packaging. It wasn't a cream but a black fold-out mask. I put it on. I lay down on the bed and placed one cucumber slice over one eye and then another on the other. I stayed like that for a while. My face slightly tingled. It was boring. I took the cucumber slices off, rolled onto my side and looked at my phone.

My boyfriend had uploaded a photo of himself, naked, his back to the camera, standing before a waterfall, his olive skin soft against jagged, volcanic rock. There were comments made by attractive people.

I knew he had a camera with a self-timer and a tripod, but the angle wasn't right. I wanted to ask who took the photo but I didn't. Instead I double-tapped it. I gave it a like.

Slowly, I felt a burning. At first it was the kind you feel when you peroxide your hair. That sensation on the scalp. It intensified. I tore the mask off.

In the bathroom I gagged. My face was slightly pink but the lump was larger and had a big yellow head. I told myself not to touch it. I touched it—it leaked.

I panicked. This was after midnight. I took the elevator to the foyer and ordered an Uber to the hospital. Drivers kept cancelling as they realised my destination. The doorman watched me. I went onto the street and hailed a taxi. The driver asked if I wanted emergency. I hesitated, then nodded. There wasn't anywhere else to go.

Outside the hospital stood women in tracksuit pants smoking cigarettes. There was a man in a white gown leaning against his IV stand. They were lit by the red emergency sign.

Inside, a toddler rolled around on the linoleum floor and an Indian couple watched something on a phone but without headphones. A studio laugh track played and played. Everyone's clothes were synthetic and cheap.

I waited in line for triage. I picked up an old fashion magazine. It was sticky. I put the magazine down.

When I got to the front I spoke to a nurse through a little perspex grille.

She said, 'What's your emergency?'

I pointed at my jaw.

'Do you have a fever?'

'No.'

'Nausea?'

'No.'

'Okay.' She leant forward to look at me. 'This is not an emergency. It's not appropriate for you to be here. You have a boil. I'm going to ask you to leave and to see your general practitioner.'

I said, 'I thought you had to see everyone.'

'That is a common misconception.' She closed the grille.

I walked the eight blocks home.

I woke up late, close to ten. The store wouldn't open till eleven. I texted Heidi to come in early, spray the room spray, prep the store. I'd be there when we opened.

Then I stood in front of the bathroom mirror and squeezed. It was like a certain kind of YouTube video. It was disgusting, full of many horrifying things.

When I was done I had to wash the mirror and wash my face. I spent a long time deciding whether or not to put toner on or apply moisturiser. The internet seemed inconclusive. I was very calm.

I texted Heidi not to open the store until I arrived. I dressed. The wound was weeping so I pressed a make-up pad on it and applied pressure.

Then Heidi replied. 'She's here.'

———

I was on the street and the icon of my Uber was moving towards me, then making turns I could not understand, and turns after those turns I understood even less. And then I was just running, my coat flaring behind me, and I thought, I am being dramatic, I am being dramatic, but I kept going and going and going. It took me ten minutes to get there, only ten minutes, and when I reached the store Heidi was standing in the doorway.

'She's gone.'

Heidi was in black kimono-like pants and a white satin collared shirt from the Spring collection. Close to dawn she'd had her hair bleached and toned. She was brilliant in the store's light.

I was still in my raincoat. I was sweating under it and the vest. I made the decision to take nothing off.

Heidi stepped out of the doorway and said, 'What happened to your face?'

There were two customers inside the store, two Asian women with designer bags. I narrowed my eyes but neither of them was R.

I said, 'What did she do?'

'She came inside. She was in all black. She looked at the store, picked a few things up, put them down. She nodded then went into the alley and her driver took her away.'

I didn't know it at the time, but later that day I would send a series of messages to my boyfriend, each message longer than the last. I would describe my life. The circumstances as I saw them. That Heidi would replace me, that others would replace me, and I would be lucky to find a position in a large department store that would play Christmas carols from the start of every November to the beginning of every January. That my good credit rating would now be a bad credit rating, but like all the times before it would slowly equalise. And that for most of my life I'd desired things I thought were stupid to desire but desired all the same.

He would reply, deep in the night, with a sad face emoji and then a photo of his penis with the caption 'Can't host', which I would understand he meant to send to someone else. This would not shock me.

But there I was, standing on the threshold of the store but not in the store.

I asked Heidi if she'd spoken to R and what R had said.

Heidi thought for a while. She kept her lips together, then opened them. 'Thank you. She said, Thank you.'

Short Stack

Sam was sitting in his living room, wearing his beige Pancake Saloon uniform, staring at the wall. He was waiting for the time when he could leave his apartment, go down the elevator four floors, cross six lanes of traffic and walk through the Saloon's employee entrance, when his phone rang. Sam didn't recognise the number but understood that someone, somewhere, wanted to speak with him. This was unusual and exciting. He answered.

'Hi there. Is that Sam? I'm Rosa.' She explained that she was calling from a collection agency without using the words collection agency. Rosa asked Sam if he remembered a particular date. He didn't. Rosa said, 'This is about your CT scan.'

On that day, Sam had had an accident. He'd been at his place of employment, taking out the trash, but sometimes the bin wasn't big enough for all the trash, so Sam had to climb into the bin and jump up and down to be able to fit in the new trash. Sam was jumping up and down but then he slipped and his vision went dark. Then shapes formed and unformed in front of him, and when he climbed out of the bin and went back into the kitchen an hour had passed and someone said, 'Hey, Sam, you're bleeding.'

Rosa explained that the insurance claim he'd filled out at the hospital was incorrect. The insurer had denied payment, so he could either send in his correct insurance details or he could pay the fee for the CT scan. The fee for the CT scan was large and frightening and depraved.

Sam said, 'I must have filled out the form wrong.'

And Rosa said, 'That's what I thought. That's what I told everyone: he must have filled out the form wrong.'

Sam said he'd gone to the hospital because he'd hit his head, so his head must have been a little funny, and Rosa said, in a soft voice, almost a whisper, 'Oh no,' and then, louder, 'Great, well, we'll need you to fill in a new form and we can clear this up.' And Sam said, 'Great,' then quickly, 'Clear this up.' Then Sam got off the phone.

Later, washing dishes at the Pancake Saloon, Sam remembered that he did not have the insurance form. Then he remembered that even if he had the insurance form he wouldn't know where to send it. This was okay, Sam thought—ideal, really, because Sam did not have insurance.

Sam was nineteen and still had baby fat and maybe some real fat and couldn't enter bars without pulling out his wallet and repeating his birthdate and star sign. The Pancake Saloon was a suburban restaurant in a franchise chain that twenty-four hours a day, seven days a week, sold pancakes drenched in concentrated high-fructose corn syrup. The restaurant had a western theme, with saloon-style doors, tables with chipped laminate designed to look like dark polished wood, and fixtures imitating nineteenth-century gas lamps that saturated the dining floor in dim, syrupy light. It was staffed exclusively by under-twenty-five-year-olds, its kitchen manned by Nepali migrants on temporary work visas.

Sam worked nights, eleven-hour shifts in the kitchen, not the restaurant. He didn't cook or make coffee or speak Nepali; he washed dishes, and at times was good at it: stacking glasses in the commercial-grade machine, blasting syrup off plates with a high-pressure nozzle, scrubbing the rubber mats that lined the floor. He was early to work, kept his uniform ironed and was overly enthusiastic in a way most people mistook as a sign of mild developmental problems.

At times, Sam fucked up. Sam fucked up especially on weekends, in the early hours of the morning, 1 a.m., 3 a.m., when the night bus ferrying drunk people from clubs and bars in the city back to their suburban homes would unload at the stop directly in front of the Pancake Saloon. All of a sudden the restaurant would be full, and the customers, often people Sam had gone to school with but who were now in college, were loud and aggressive. They'd empty packets of sugar and cartons of creamer onto tables, vomit in toilet stalls, even perform partially clothed sex acts in open booths. The ambient pressure, almost barometric, moved into the kitchen, and Sam would begin to work in a kind of slow motion. Sam put clean dishes in the dishwasher and moved behind people without saying 'behind', causing people to trip, vats of thick pancake batter to spill and the cooks to loudly repeat the Nepali word for idiot.

Then, after four, there would be calm, and by five, when the night manager left to do the night's cash drop, the floor staff would sit on milk crates behind the restaurant, next to the skip, and smoke weed, and though no one offered Sam weed, Sam would sit with them or stand in their vicinity. Servers would say things like, 'I think the Pancake Saloon should blow up,' or, 'There should be a flood and the flood should wash away the Pancake Saloon.' And as people got higher they would become more inventive. 'There should be a flood and the flood washes away the Pancake Saloon but there's a gas explosion and as the Pancake Saloon washes away it's also on fire.' And Sam would say, 'The Pancake Saloon sucks.' Not because he thought it sucked but because he wanted to contribute. He liked the Pancake Saloon. He liked it a lot.

If someone asked Sam when he was happiest—no one did, but he held the answer close to him in case the question ever came up in some online survey or chain Facebook post or interview for an unspecified higher position—he would say he was happiest eating a stack of pancakes drenched in high-fructose corn syrup. He was happiest eating them at the Pancake Saloon with his friends who were not his friends but his co-workers.

Sam came home from work, entering his small economy apartment close to dawn. He showered, then moved around the living room in the near dark.

His apartment was on the fourth floor of a shoddily constructed tower that sat at the intersection of two main roads, one with six lanes, the other eight. The former connected the suburbs to the city, and the latter was a freeway linking the greater metropolitan northeast to the greater metropolitan east. His apartment consisted of a small bedroom, an en suite bathroom and a living room. From his living room, Sam could look out across the lanes of traffic and see the Westfield mall and, further down, the Pancake Saloon, its neon sign forty feet high, a stack of pancakes blinking on and off in the night.

Sam played PlayStation and felt slightly sad. Before the shift change, as people sat on crates outside, Sam had asked if people wanted to chill at his place. One by one, Sam had asked Simon and Sam had asked Becca and Sam had asked Ryan if they wanted to come back to his place, and no one said yes but instead, 'Maybe next time,' though he had been told 'Maybe next time' many times before.

Playing PlayStation, Sam imagined everyone kicking on to his apartment, where people would comment on his things and say, That's a cool TV, or, Wow, is that the espresso machine George Clooney uses? and in Sam's imagination, Sam saw himself—toggled to third-person view—making espressos for everyone, except as he spoke and used the espresso machine he didn't look quite like Sam but like Sam if Sam were also George Clooney, or like George Clooney if George Clooney were actually Sam.

Sam had other nice things in his apartment, some more visible and some less so. He had a Visa Platinum card and an Amex Ultimate card, as well as a defaulted payment plan for a personal loan he had optimistically taken out a year earlier for an ill-conceived trip to Japan, where he had felt largely alienated, the language barrier difficult, and had eaten a variety of foods, mainly pancakes shaped and coloured to look like different foods. The defaulted payment plan wasn't physically visible in the apartment except for the fact that when he was in Japan he had used a part of the loan to purchase and take home, through customs, for reasons now opaque to him, a full-size katana. He'd then hung the katana in its fluorescent green sheath on his living room wall. When Sam looked up from playing PlayStation and saw the sword he didn't think, That's my defaulted payment plan, but rather, That is a sweet sword. Then he went back to feeling alone.

Sam woke at noon. Sam worked six days out of seven, and if he was asked to work on the seventh he said yes. Today was Sam's day off and on Sam's days off he didn't know exactly what he should do.

He got up, looked at the Pancake Saloon from his window, wondered what people were doing inside, then left his apartment for the mall, where he bought a large juice that was not predominantly juice but sugar and frozen yogurt, and walked from one side of the mall to the other. He walked quickly, with purpose, his arms pressed against his sides, like he was rushing to meet someone, a group of friends, a date. When he got to the end of the mall, a large, cavernous food court, he turned around and circled back.

The mall was filled with teenagers who still went to school. When Sam still went to school he'd been excited to leave it. Though he wasn't bullied, Sam had not had many friends in high school and imagined the time after it to be one in which he'd interact with many people and all these people would like him and want to do things with him. He would smile and these people would smile and it would be like in an advertisement in which small products, an opened bottle of soda or unwrapped candy bar, lead to spontaneous parties and beaches and fun. Sam thought the Pancake Saloon was a little bit like this but actually not like this at all.

Back at his apartment, Sam entered his windowless bedroom and lay on the bed. He was bored. He put some music on. Then he opened his laptop and watched an eighteen-year-old boy sit on a swivel chair and masturbate in real time. This was on a site that had previously saved Sam's credit card details.

Sam's credit card was charged to buy tokens, and Sam could then give away these tokens. For differing amounts the boys on the screen would dance, angle their web-cams lower, pull down their underwear and put things in and out of their bodies while touching themselves. Sam tipped but was careful not to tip too much, because if he tipped too much the performer might climax and then quickly log off.

Sam was watching a cam boy he often watched, ShyGuy18, because ShyGuy18 was friendly, had supposedly once been shy like Sam, and often interacted with viewers. He was thin, had hair the colour of aqua-blue bubble gum, and cammed from a small, carpeted bedroom somewhere in Virginia, a light projector making faint disco patterns across the walls.

Sam could interact with him by typing messages. Sam thought that if ShyGuy18 and Sam lived in the same city they would be friends. Sam often typed messages into the chat window and ShyGuy18 would talk to him, or not to him specifically but to the chat room as a whole. He would talk about his day and then send links. It was kind of like hanging out at the mall because the links would take Sam to the world's largest mall, Amazon, to ShyGuy18's wish list, a large, white screen where you could scroll across product icons and buy the things he wanted. The list was similar to other cam boy wish lists—better recording equipment, a swivel chair made to look like the seat of a race car, sex toys, the latest *Grand Theft Auto*—but also included more original requests: a Mixmaster, tropical fish, an officially licensed *SpongeBob SquarePants* Pineapple House aquarium ornament.

Sam bought ShyGuy18 the *SpongeBob SquarePants* Pineapple House and then typed, 'I bought you the Pineapple House,' into the chat window and ShyGuy18 said, 'Yay,' and then he spoke to Sam by name—not Sam's real name but Sam's username. He said, 'Thank you, shortstack2013.' Sam blushed. Every now and then Sam tipped him and his browser made a sound of coins falling and Sam felt happy. Then it was over, and Sam was alone again in his apartment.

He left his bedroom. It was dark outside. It was ten.

Sam could tell whether or not the Pancake Saloon was busy by counting the number of cars in the lot. He could count them, standing there, looking out from his living room window. The lot was full. Sam called his manager and asked if they needed anyone to come in tonight. Sam's manager said no.

Hours passed. When Sam spent too much time alone he thought of himself in a series of adjectives, rapidly cycling between *helpful, friendly* and *slightly obese*.

Rosa called again. She asked how Sam was. She asked about his financial situation, and Sam misinterpreted this as her taking an interest in his life. Sam described the Pancake Saloon in great detail. Rosa absently said, 'Okay, okay,' then asked Sam if he had insurance.

Sam didn't like to lie to people who were kind to him. He said he didn't have insurance.

Rosa said she was glad he had told her. Rosa explained, again, that Sam would need to pay for the CT scan. The CT scan was three thousand dollars. Rosa asked if Sam understood her. Sam nodded. The line was quiet. Then Sam said, 'Oh, I nodded,' and Rosa said, 'Great.'

At the Pancake Saloon, Sam stood in front of the manager's office door and waited. Sam didn't want to knock on the door but to seem to be there coincidentally when his manager came out. Sam's manager, Kelly, was twenty-four and would sometimes sit on a milk crate smoking with everyone and say, 'The Pancake Saloon should blow up,' and other times would yell at them to work harder. It was variable, and like Kelly's frequently changing hair colour had to do with things happening, unseen, in Kelly's personal life.

When Kelly came out of the office Sam asked if he could have shifts during the day. Kelly said they already had a dishwasher during the day, and Sam said, 'Okay,' and then Kelly said they needed a server. Sam said he could be a server.

Kelly paused then said, 'Yeah, whatever.' And then, 'You'd be working double shifts, though.' Sam said this was fine.

Sam went back to the kitchen and imagined all the money he would make as a server. He imagined his rapport with customers, then imagined having regulars. Sam imagined serving his regulars and his regulars going on to have lovely days because Sam had served them.

He was so excited that when he got home he felt like he couldn't sleep, so he didn't. He waited for the mall to open and then, to celebrate, walked to EB Games, where he bought himself the latest *Grand Theft Auto*. He thought he shouldn't spend money but then he thought that it was important to celebrate when things were worth celebrating. When you got a promotion, you should celebrate. That wasn't a bad thing to do.

At the register, Sam's credit card was declined. Sam took out another card.

During Sam's first shift in the dining room, his customers were not particularly friendly. They were like the non-player characters in *Grand Theft Auto*: impatient and said rude things when Sam accidentally bumped into them.

It was a weekday shift and that meant it was slow, though it didn't feel slow to Sam. Moving through the dining room, Sam felt his inner voice take on the tone of a reality-television chef who visits people's restaurants to yell at them about how shittily they run their restaurants. The voice swore at him to be better, to be faster, and because the voice swore at him he made stupid mistakes. He took orders to the wrong tables, he got confused with substitutions, he poured non-decaf coffee into a mug half-filled with decaf. When people complained he said, 'I don't know,' 'Beats me,' 'That's weird.' When a family said they wanted to talk to a manager, he said, 'That's okay,' and then, 'Your meals are free.'

Sam's manager, the daytime manager, the franchise owner's son, told Sam to come into his office. The manager was in his twenties, tanned, and sometimes took money for cigarettes directly from the register. The office was a small, windowless room crowded with a desktop computer, four large filing cabinets the colour of pancake batter and the Saloon's security safe. The manager told Sam that he could not comp people's meals. 'That's bad business.'

Sam said, 'Okay.' Then Sam stood on the dining room floor and his reality-television-chef inner voice gave him orders using sporting metaphors that Sam didn't fully understand. The voice said, 'Step up to the fucking plate,' 'Knock it out of the park,' 'Fucking call the shots.'

At Sam's apartment building, in Sam's mailbox, was a letter. It was from Amex. His card's credit limit had been increased.

Between Sam's day shift and night shift he watched Shy-Guy18's cam show, used his Amex to buy gifts off ShyGuy18's Amazon wish list—a Sunbeam Mixmaster, an LED ring light—then played *Grand Theft Auto*. He played through the opening scene, a bank robbery and a car chase, then found himself with a fresh start in a vast computer-generated city, an open world. Sam didn't like doing missions or following the story as the missions were boring and often difficult, and Sam didn't like killing people because it didn't seem very nice.

What Sam did always do was run out onto the street and steal a car—it didn't have to be a good car; it could be a Toyota Camry that for licensing reasons in-game was not a Toyota Camry—then drive on the freeway towards the horizon. He toggled the radio until he hit the all-pop, all-hits channel, then cruised.

When Sam felt particularly pumped up or aspirational he would try to steal a private jet. But it was hard to steal a private jet, because driving onto the airport's airfield brought a lot of heat, and to deal with that heat required a level of coordination with the PlayStation controller that Sam lacked, so he would usually get arrested or killed. Sometimes Sam paused the game to watch a YouTube tutorial on how to hijack a private jet, and in the YouTube tutorial it seemed easy: the player should simply approach the jet. As the uploader, a teenage boy, approached, he said, 'Yeah, yeah. This is what everyone wants. Grey Goose, baby. Private planes.'

That wasn't really what Sam wanted. As Sam played, he would think of a minigame in one of the old *Grand Theft Auto*s in which you could drive a scooter and deliver pizzas or takeaway noodles. In some games you could even enter fast-food restaurants and order a burger and fries. Sam thought it would be funny if, in this latest *Grand Theft Auto*, he could work at a Pancake Saloon. He could come home from work, open his save file then have his character do a shift at the Pancake Saloon, entering through a 3D-rendered employee entrance, wearing a uniform identical to Sam's, and then come back to his crib, which would be filled with all the cool shit Sam would buy.

That was what Sam wanted.

Sam answered calls and the calls were Rosa. Rosa was very understanding and said things like, 'I understand.' Rosa said she would email paperwork for a payment plan but that it was very important that Sam mail the signed paperwork back. Sam said he would send the paperwork back, and then when it arrived, he thought, I don't have a printer. Sam thought maybe he could use the printer in the Pancake Saloon's office. Sam visualised doing this, walking in and booting up the manager's computer, printing and signing the paperwork, the things he would say if the manager came into the office. He would say something like, Oh, hey. Because Sam imagined each of these actions so vividly he then didn't do any of them. When Sam remembered he hadn't, he'd think, Well, I don't have a printer.

Other collectors called Sam. These were for his personal loan and his Visa card, but not yet his Amex. Sam was in his apartment. He added the figures together. Sam spent almost half of his pay cheque on rent and bought groceries on credit, because when he used credit he also got points. The savings on the points were significantly less than the losses to interest, but Sam didn't fully understand this. He worked day and night. What Sam understood was that he needed more money. He needed more income.

Between work and playing PlayStation, Sam thought that he could monetise his other activities, like touching himself while watching other people touch themselves online. Sam could cam. Clicking through the cam site's rooms, less out of sexual interest than to fill time, Sam knew there wasn't one single thing people wanted but a multitude, and in that multitude, someone, somewhere, might want him. They would want him and want to be his friend. They would say, You are amazing, You're so cute, Take my money. Sam imagined stacks of crisp bills.

The thought made him giggle.

Sam sat on his couch and set up his laptop on the coffee table. He used his Amex card to upgrade his membership from viewer to performer. For a moment it looked like the payment wouldn't clear, but then it did. Sam angled the screen up and opened his room.

The room's name was the same as his username, short-stack2013. Sam saw himself and his apartment on the screen. On the webcam, Sam's economy apartment looked like an economy apartment. He looked at the resolution and thought his apartment would look better in high definition and that he should invest in a better webcam—that is, if he wanted to do this professionally.

Sam put on a black ski mask he had bought and then never worn on his trip to Japan. He put the ski mask on because he was shy and thought the ski mask might be liberating, and to viewers erotic. His lips and eyes were visible. He took his Pancake Saloon shirt off but felt self-conscious so put it back on. He placed his arms across his chest. He thought that ShyGuy18 must also be shy, but ShyGuy18 had worked past it and seemed to have a good time. He thought he shouldn't think too much about what he was doing, and just be spontaneous.

Sam put his feet up on the coffee table in a way that was suggestive. He took his socks off. Then he put his socks back on, thinking he'd take them off when there were viewers. There were feeds on the site where boys were tipped to sit on a couch while another boy massaged their big feet, sucked on their toes. That seemed okay to Sam. That seemed easy. But Sam did not have big feet. Or someone to suck on them.

He put on some music and kind of nodded his head. It was exciting. He was exciting. He thought about all the products he would put on his own Amazon wish list once he'd settled his debt. He saw each product in front of him, floating, suspended in empty white space.

Sam's browser made a noise. A viewer had entered the room. Sam tried to make a sexy face by thinking, Sexy face, and pouted his lips through the mask. Then Sam stood up, inhaled, and began to lift his shirt. Slowly he exhaled. His belly filled the screen and resembled, more than anything, a smooth milk bun. His viewer was watching. Sam stepped from side to side. Then Sam lowered his underwear. Sam stood still. His laptop made another noise, a different noise, a kind of sad noise. Sam said, 'Hello,' then realised his one viewer had left the room.

Weeks passed. When Sam answered the phone it was Rosa but it wasn't Rosa. It was Bad Cop Rosa. Bad Cop Rosa said mean things. She said, 'Pay the money.' She said, 'I don't care. Pay up!' She said, 'You're in a bad situation. You're going to go to court.' She yelled, 'Compound interest!'

Sam owed $6000 on his Visa card and $4500 on his Amex. $5600 remained on his personal loan, and then there was the cost of the CT scan. Plus interest. This was all unconsolidated.

At work Sam told the daytime manager that he thought the Pancake Saloon should cover or help cover the cost of his CT scan.

The daytime manager said, 'What?' and Sam said, 'From the time I fell at work.'

The manager asked if Sam had filed an incident report.

'I don't know,' Sam said.

'So how can the Pancake Saloon know you actually hurt yourself working?' Sam's manager said. 'To allege that you injured yourself here, so the Pancake Saloon pays for your personal medical fees, well, that's a serious allegation. That's not the kind of Pancake Saloon employee this Pancake Saloon employs.'

Sam said, 'It was at work.'

Sam's manager said, 'Go back to your tables.' And that's what Sam did.

Later, at home, he sat in his living room, lit by the television's glow. Sam didn't have a shift that night and felt a kind of restlessness he associated with drinking too many energy drinks or espressos from his espresso machine. He played *Grand Theft Auto*. He drove across one freeway then merged onto another, weaving between traffic.

It was late, past three. He gripped the controller and stood up, looked at the Pancake Saloon through the window, then sat back down. Occasionally thoughts raced through Sam's mind, and the thoughts raced so quickly they left ghost trails. The thoughts were: MONEY, Money, money, and CASH, Cash, cash.

Fuck the Pancake Saloon, Sam thought. If the Pancake Saloon were in *Grand Theft Auto* he would use a rocket launcher to blow it up. He would plough an SUV through the Pancake Saloon's front windows. Though if the Pancake Saloon were in *Grand Theft Auto* the rocket would explode on the Pancake Saloon's exterior and the SUV would hit it and then bounce off. The buildings in *Grand Theft Auto* were indestructible.

Sam turned the PlayStation off. From his living room window, Sam realised, he could watch the night manager,

Kelly, walk from the Saloon to the bank to deposit the night's takings. It would be close to five. His eyes could follow Kelly leaving the restaurant from the employee entrance, waiting for the traffic light, crossing the six lanes to get to the mall, then walking alongside the mall's parking lot, shadows lengthening under the streetlights, until she stopped at the bank's deposit chute.

The restaurant had strict procedures that were written up in the Pancake Saloon's employee manuals. When the night shift made the cash drop, two people were meant to take it: the night manager and someone else. But the Pancake Saloon that Sam worked in was a franchise, where the approach, especially at night, when the owner's son wasn't there, had, over time, been replaced with a new one, which was to follow the corporate procedures as little as possible. Kelly took the money alone.

Sam thought he could take that money. Sam imagined this as a mission in *Grand Theft Auto*. Sam would cover his face with his ski mask, then at 4 a.m. go downstairs and wait in the mall's parking lot. He would wait for Kelly to cross the road, and then, before she reached the bank chute, leap out from the dark.

Sam would speak in a low voice. Maybe even use one of those machines that you press against your throat, a voice changer or vocoder. Sam would say, Give me the money. Sam would speak like a gangster from *Grand Theft Auto* if the gangster were also using a vocoder. He'd say, Give me the money, bitch, and raise a fake gun. Sam realised he didn't have a fake gun, so in Sam's imagination he was holding his katana, still in its sheath. He would wave the katana and say bitch a few times. Then Sam would grab the money. Then Sam would run.

This scene was followed by a quick montage: Sam in his apartment, counting money, counting so much money, more money than the Pancake Saloon would make in one night. Sam at work, unsuspected, later that day. Sam's debts being settled. Sam buying himself nice things. Sam living his life.

But Sam wouldn't do this, any of this, because Sam was bad at missions and knew that if he tried he would fuck it up, or he might scare Kelly, and he didn't want to scare Kelly, or Kelly might scare him and pull out a canister of mace.

Sam accepted this. Sam's heart beat rapidly in the dark.

At work there was an incident. During the morning rush a woman had come in with two children. If the woman were in *Grand Theft Auto* she would be a character walking on the street in the business district. She wore a suit.

Sam brought the woman her order: three plates of pancakes smothered in high-fructose corn syrup and a coffee.

The woman said, 'I've made a request, and it was a simple request, and you haven't done it. My daughter wanted ice cream.'

Sam picked up one of the plates and said he would add a scoop of ice cream.

'Make them fresh. The pancakes should be fresh.'

Sam said, 'Yes.' Sam said he would go to the kitchen and be right back.

In the kitchen Sam put the plate of pancakes under the heat lamp. Sam waited a few minutes then asked if someone else could take the pancakes to his table. No one replied.

Sam put a scoop of ice cream onto the pancakes and returned to the dining room with the order. He set it down.

The woman sipped her coffee, then let the coffee fall out of her mouth and back into the cup. She wiped her lips with a paper napkin. She said, 'This coffee is tepid.'

Sam said he would replace the coffee.

'It isn't about the coffee,' she said. 'It's about the level of service. I was having a good day and now I'm having a bad one. My children are having a bad time.' The children seemed happy. They were doing what Sam wished he were doing: eating pancakes.

'Do you understand?' the woman said. The woman spoke to Sam like she thought Sam had made poor life choices and she was personally offended by those choices. She communicated that she was training her children to be members of society, members who would not serve people pancakes, or have debt, or if they did have debt they would have the good kind of debt, the kind that could be leveraged.

Sam said, 'That's okay,' and the woman said, 'No, it's not okay,' and Sam said, 'Your meals are free.'

When they finished eating they walked past the register and into the parking lot. Sam watched them through the Saloon's plate glass getting into their car, an expensive car, the woman buckling the smaller child into a safety seat. They drove away.

The daytime manager was standing behind Sam. The daytime manager said, 'Did you just comp their meal?'

Sam was asked to leave. At home Sam lay in bed. Sam watched ShyGuy18's cam show but didn't have any tokens, so Sam sat and looked at ShyGuy18, and ShyGuy18, shirtless, seemed to look through his webcam and through

Sam's screen, making eye contact, and ShyGuy18's eyes were communicating, and what they were saying was, Tip me, but Sam couldn't. His cards had maxed out. Sam typed 'Hello' into the chat window and ShyGuy18 stood up and half-pulled his underwear down then pulled the underwear back up. Sam typed, 'How are you?' ShyGuy18 sat on his swivel chair for a while, then got up and left the room. In the corner of the room Sam saw a small aquarium. Inside the aquarium was an officially licensed *SpongeBob SquarePants* Pineapple House ornament. ShyGuy18 came back with a Coke Zero. Sam wrote, 'I had a bad day.' ShyGuy18 concentrated on the can of Coke Zero, then on the screen, and then on something off-screen. ShyGuy18 typed, 'I'll cam later.' The feed cut to black.

Sam received calls from unlisted numbers. They called in the morning, the afternoon, the dead of night. Sam's debt was sold to one collection agency, then to another. His debt was swapped and traded alongside other people's debt like Yu-Gi-Oh! cards. Sometimes Sam answered the calls, sometimes he didn't. When he did answer he would say, 'I cannot take your call right now. I am at my place of employment,' and they would say, 'Pay us the fucking money!' and Sam would say, 'Goodbye,' disconnecting the call with a kind of giddiness, his heart beating fast, then slow, then fast again, until the feeling faded away.

Sam was no longer a server. This made sense to him—he was a terrible server. Sam still worked at the Pancake Saloon washing dishes. Sometimes as Sam sprayed dishes his inner voice would yell, 'Bankrupt!' like he was on a game show or playing and winning a variant of Yahtzee. At certain shift intervals he mopped the kitchen floor.

When Sam got home from his shifts, he placed his phone in his fridge's vegetable crisper then played *Grand Theft Auto*. Sam had got better at *Grand Theft Auto*. Sam stole a car and drove to the airport. Sam wanted a private jet. There was a chase. Explosions. Multi-car pile-ups.

Almost every time Sam died, but then one time he didn't. He drove through the mass of concrete that was the airport and reached the private jet. He jumped in. He floored the jet's engines, police officers running across the tarmac, SWAT team members in helicopters, bullets raining down. And then the jet was on the runway and the jet was moving faster and faster. It began to lift.

Sam was in the air. Then the city was below him, all its freeways and fast-food restaurants and shitty apartment towers like Sam's shitty apartment tower, and a calm came over him. He angled the plane up, flying higher and higher, until the altitude maxed and the game's draw distance glitched, and each direction, above and below, collapsed into sky.

Charlie in
High Definition

The cat behavioural specialist was in Houston. She appeared via video link on Emma's MacBook. Emma and Dan sat in Fort Greene, Brooklyn, in their apartment's living room. They lived on the fourth floor of a walk-up. Prewar. It was light out, late afternoon. From their windows they could see the tops of oaks, branches beginning to bud with leaves, and, across the street, a woman rummaging through trash.

The cat behavioural specialist was seated in front of a white wall. She wore a crewneck sweater, had short blonde hair and glasses Emma could tell were cheap. She looked striking.

The specialist asked questions. Emma picked up the cat and held him in front of the MacBook. The specialist repeated the cat's name: 'Charlie.' Dan tried to angle Charlie's face towards the camera and the specialist said, 'Stop doing that.'

Charlie began to squirm. He was heavy. Charlie was black, part Maine Coon, and so large that Dan had once bought a leash and harness from PetSmart only to return and exchange it for one advertised for medium-to-large dogs.

They had used the leash once to take Charlie to the park, where Charlie had yowled and hyperventilated until they carried him home.

Emma let go of Charlie. The specialist said, 'When did the problem start?'

Before the video call, Emma and Dan had discussed what details they would and would not include. They had a list.

Emma spoke. She was trying to be as clear and concise as possible, but Emma also thought Dan, who had been sceptical about hiring the specialist, might make a joke while she explained the problem, and if Dan made a joke Emma would be irritated, and so she became irritated thinking about how Dan was distracting her by making or not making a joke. Emma lost her train of thought.

After a pause, she said, 'A month or so ago, I don't know, there was a cat on the fire escape and Charlie didn't like the cat being there. He hissed at it. The other cat thought it was funny. It kept walking up and down the fire escape then looking at Charlie through the window. The cat was mocking him.' Emma remembered this was something she and Dan had deemed not relevant. Emma said, 'Probably not relevant.'

The specialist nodded then described an article she had read online. Emma was listening and typing what the specialist said into her phone. The article was about a woman who fainted in an airplane bathroom, broke her ankle then blamed the airline for failing to supply her with enough water. She had fainted, she believed, due to dehydration. Before take-off the woman had asked a flight attendant for water, and the attendant had left and not come back. She was suing for damages. The woman claimed the incident had caused ongoing problems which led to her withdrawing from her social circle, and also to the dissolution of her fifteen-year marriage. The airline's lawyers said that there were drinking fountains throughout the plane that passengers could drink from at any time, and the woman's lawyer said the woman did not know about the drinking fountains.

'It's a tough one. I mean, who can say?' the specialist said. 'Do you understand?'

Emma did not.

The specialist said, 'We're trying to understand behaviour.'

Emma was teaching when the issue started. Emma adjuncted, teaching one studio class for a Digital Arts major at a college's satellite campus nestled in the woods of Long Island. The studio classes were held late in the afternoon, in a large computer lab, each class a three-hour block that stretched into evening.

Emma made digital and mixed media installations that had been shown in New York, Montreal, Berlin and, at one point, Seoul. She'd taken the adjunct role a year ago after one of her former professors approached her with an opening at his new college.

A lecturer there, an artist whose work Emma was familiar with, had sent a unit results email to his students with the subject line 're: sluts'. People were offended. Students made allegations of a certain culture. The man stated that there had been an issue with his phone's autocorrect. The incident came to dominate the department and involved an extended mediation between the department, the lecturer, the student body and HR, culminating in a series of faculty-wide emails, the last containing an obscene computer-generated video created and sent by the now former lecturer.

'All you have to do,' Emma's former professor told her, 'is take the studio class and not be crazy.'

Emma replied, 'I am not crazy,' and was given the job. This all happened while she looked for something else but then found she couldn't really do something else, something full-time, while she also taught.

Emma's phone was off. Though the studio class didn't ban phones—students could use theirs if they needed to—Emma liked to set an example. Emma's phone was in her bag. Her voicemail was filling with messages. Frantic messages, then terse ones. Emma sat at the front of the studio, facing her students, who faced their computers, or, more often, faced each other.

She ended the studio seven minutes early. During the studio, students had moved their chairs to sit with friends. The students were meant to move their chairs back at the end, but they didn't. Emma did, then went to the adjunct office where she had a desk that was not really her desk but was her desk between 6 and 7 p.m. every Thursday night. In this, her office hour, she was meant to see students or, if there were no students, catch up on administration. Normally this hour was empty time punctuated by her standing up, crossing the hall to the staffroom, making a weak instant coffee, crossing the hallway back to her office and sitting in the office staring at a college-branded poster that read 'The Future is Female' while not really understanding what this meant.

She took out her phone and saw seven missed calls. There were also text messages. These were all from Emma and Dan's new roommate. This roommate, Amber, had only been in the apartment five nights. Emma called her. Amber whispered that she was trapped—she couldn't leave the bathroom. The cat wouldn't let her. Emma said, 'Charlie?' And Amber said, 'Yes.'

Emma said, 'Let me try and reach Dan.' Emma got off the phone. She called Dan. He didn't answer. Thursday nights he had after-work drinks with the other graphic designers at his agency. Usually Emma came home to him lying on their comforter saying, 'I'm not drunk,' then whispering softly, 'Maybe a little drunk.'

It would take almost two hours to commute home from Long Island. Emma messaged Amber that she was on her way.

When Emma arrived at the apartment, Charlie greeted her, purring, brushing himself against her legs. Amber was still inside the bathroom. Emma knocked on the door.

Amber explained that she had been in the hallway taking off her coat when the cat hissed at her, began to chase her, and then once she was barricaded in the bathroom she could see his shadow, pacing, on the other side of the door. After an hour Amber had peeked out only to see Charlie tilt his head up at her, open his fangs wide and scream.

'What do you mean, scream?' Emma said.

'I mean he screamed.'

Emma apologised. Charlie was rolling on the floor at Emma's feet.

Amber said, 'He was being an asshole,' and stepped over the cat. Amber went to her room.

When Dan came home he and Emma spoke about it, but not for long. Dan laughed. It seemed like just a weird thing that had happened and because it seemed like just a weird thing that had happened it was easy to feel that it hadn't happened at all.

In bed, Emma wore headphones and typed 'cat screaming' into her phone. She wore headphones because she didn't want Charlie, who was nestled against her thigh, to become agitated. Dan turned off the light and tried to sleep. In bed, they didn't sleep touching each other. Dan thought Emma fidgeted. Emma did fidget but because she was often awake. Emma lowered her screen's brightness then watched one video after another. She let them run on autoplay. The cats distended their jaws. The cats screamed.

Emma wasn't thinking about this the next morning. Dan left for work and Emma lingered in bed, Charlie still asleep, spooning her calf with one paw. Eventually she got up to work.

Emma taught at the college but predominantly did freelance work producing renders for a few independent architects and interior designers, all small projects: an upstate bungalow, a penthouse terrace. Clients sent her SketchUp models, then she would make the simulated environments, render them, and for a larger fee, build for VR.

Most of her work was done at home, at her desk in the back corner of the living room. Emma's arrangement could be described as 'flexible', though often it seemed like Emma was always working and none of it was art. There hadn't been a point at which Emma decided she wasn't making art anymore, she just wasn't making art at this time. This time had been the past three years.

Emma showered and dressed. She did what she did every day and left the apartment to buy a six-dollar coffee from the coffee shop a block down. Because she'd stayed up late she ordered two, saving one to reheat later in the day.

She was back at her desk when Charlie came into the room, but wouldn't settle. Charlie was gentle and sociable but could also be very needy. At times this made it challenging for Emma to get work done. Charlie jumped onto the desk and then jumped off the desk.

Emma edited a render, shifted things, adjusted code.

Emma maybe wasn't happy with her life but Emma loved the apartment and her life within the apartment. The apartment had two bedrooms, high ceilings, long windows, and floorboards that in some places were buckled and warped but in a way that was charming, Parisian. During the day the light was diffuse, the air as luminous as one of her renders. When they had signed the lease Emma and Dan had painted the walls fresh white, then filled the apartment with beautiful things.

Soon after moving it became apparent that they couldn't afford the apartment alone. They burned through money. Owned no assets. Dan had student loans. Emma had student loans.

Acknowledging this, they rented the second bedroom, a very cramped room, on Airbnb. This resulted in the co-op board sending an email to all tenants complaining about increased foot traffic, and in particular people rolling luggage through the foyer and up the stairs. And then their realtor had given them an official warning to immediately desist, using bullet points, listing the ways in which their use of Airbnb violated the terms of their lease. Emma and Dan did not admit they were renting the room on Airbnb. The realtor sent them screenshots of their listing. They stopped renting the room.

After this, for five months they sublet the room to an NYU student named Atar. When he had moved in, his parents helped. They'd asked Emma and Dan if they were married. When Dan said no, they spoke—Emma thought heatedly—in Punjabi and then left the apartment. Atar mainly stayed in his room, drank 32 oz cans of Monster and did things on the internet. When Emma and Dan went away, Atar looked after Charlie. They paid him by leaving him ziplock bags of weed. Then Atar moved out, and there were others, and now the room was Amber's.

At two, Emma heard Amber come out of her bedroom into the kitchen and pause on the way back. Emma thought Amber might make conversation, but then, relieved, she heard Amber go back to her room. Emma hadn't wanted Amber as their new roommate because she was another student, and Emma didn't like what that implied: that she was living with the people she taught or that she herself was still in college. Once Amber's door had shut, Emma got up and reheated her second coffee.

Charlie stretched then followed her, strutting in a deliberate way. He did this when he wanted food. Because he was black and fluffy his back legs resembled parachute pants, narrow at the paws and wide everywhere else. This was heightened when Charlie engaged in his strut. Emma called this 'Runway Charlie'.

She ignored him. She came back to her desk and sent a client email. She did more work. She read the client's reply. It was five.

Emma closed her MacBook, stood up and put wine from the fridge into a tote bag. Then the picnic blanket. 'Runway Charlie' began to meow. She fed him. When Dan got home they would walk to the park, meet friends, and even though it was cold, sit and drink as the sun set. Emma waited.

Emma and Dan were sitting in Fort Greene Park. It was dark, the Martyrs' Monument already lit with floodlights. They were with friends. They were discussing going to an Indian restaurant. One of their friends had a dog. They were discussing dropping the dog at the owner's apartment and then walking together to the restaurant. Emma was drinking quickly to feel warm, but subtly, on the down-low.

Her phone vibrated. It was Amber. Emma answered. Amber was speaking fast. It was loud at the park. Emma walked away from the picnic blanket.

The cat had attacked her, Amber said. The cat attacked her. Emma could hear a terrible sound in the background. She recognised the sound. It was a scream. Emma got off the phone.

Emma told everyone she had to go. She broke, dramatically she thought, into a run. Then she stopped running and walked, but a fast walk. Dan caught up to her.

When they entered the apartment there was blood on the floorboards. Charlie was standing at Amber's door, his fur all puffed up. They shut him in the bathroom. Amber didn't want to come out but she let Emma come in.

Amber was pantless. A series of cuts ran up one leg. She had left the house to buy a pre-packaged salad and when she'd returned, as she was taking the salad back to her room, from the hallway the cat had pounced, letting out a great scream, and attached himself to her right shin, then, thrashing his claws, climbed onto her thigh. Somehow Amber had shaken him off and made it to her room.

She had been wearing rigid vintage Levi's, and Charlie's claws had cut through the denim and into flesh.

Emma went to the bathroom and, careful not to let Charlie out, gathered gauze, antiseptic cream. Emma treated Amber's leg. As she pressed gauze on the cuts they would turn pale, but when she relieved the pressure the cuts would bloom. This made Emma begin to panic, but then the cuts looked okay. She dressed them.

Amber said, 'This is fucked up.'

That same night, to make it seem like things were changing, they took Charlie to the vet.

They sat at the animal hospital with the cat carrier on the floor draped with a towel. A man walking a dog came to sit near them and Emma said, 'No, this is the cat area. Go to the dog area.' The man looked at her and she pointed to the sign 'Cat Waiting Area' and then he, and slowly the dog, moved away. Dan made a noise. She said, 'I'm right,' then they were called into a room.

Charlie came out of his carrier and was held by the vet, a woman in blue scrubs. They described the attack. The vet asked if the cat was injured. They said they didn't think he was, and the vet scratched Charlie's head and put him down on a small table. Charlie slowly walked across the table, then jumped down onto the linoleum floor and began to pant. Then he made a kind of honking noise and stood between Emma's legs. The vet told her that she had a very sensitive cat.

Emma explained that normally Charlie was very friendly. He had dealt with multiple strangers in the house, with some staying for more than a month. They weren't sure why his behaviour had changed.

They were told that they could give Charlie Prozac. Emma didn't think she wanted to give her cat Prozac, because Prozac suggested her cat was depressed, not just anxious, and that was hard for her to think about. It wasn't an immediate solution, the vet told them—the drug wouldn't start affecting the cat's behaviour until four weeks had passed, and it had possible side effects including cat anorexia and cat seizures. Also, for them to administer the medication the cat had to swallow pills, and tussling with him every morning to force him to swallow them might make him more aggressive, counteracting the drug's effects.

The vet asked if they roughhoused the cat. Emma knew she wasn't meant to roughhouse with Charlie, but she had done so anyway. Since he was a kitten she would sometimes run around the apartment and he would jump across furniture and she would grab him, and he would put his teeth lightly around her palm and then roll away. His behaviour with the roommate seemed different.

'No,' Emma said. 'I don't.'

Dan looked at her. Except for Charlie, who continued to make a low honking noise, they were quiet.

Emma asked if there was anything else they could do.

The vet replied, 'Try not having a roommate.'

———

At home they told Amber that things would be better, and then devised a plan in which one of them would be home in the apartment with the cat at all times unless Amber had communicated she was out.

Emma and Dan were worried that Amber would move, and if Amber did move they would need to pay back a prorated portion of rent, refund her security deposit, find a new roommate and until then cover the rent alone. This would be difficult.

Sometimes they didn't know how long Amber would be gone for and so one of them would go out for dinner and the other would stay with Charlie. Or one would go to work and one would wait for the other to come home. Because Emma could freelance theoretically anywhere, it was decided that this would for the most part be her.

Even when Emma was home, keeping Charlie and Amber separated was tricky due to the layout of the apartment. The only rooms that the cat could be kept in were the bathroom, which Amber would need to use, and their bedroom. The bedroom had certain limitations. The door would not shut unless the door was locked from the inside. This was due to a broken latch. Their super answered Emma's emails with 'I'll fix it' and then didn't fix it.

Emma couldn't work in the living room. When she did, Charlie was free to move around the apartment and when he heard the latch of Amber's door he would bolt towards it. So Emma would lock the cat and herself in the bedroom and lie on the bed with her MacBook, falling in and out of sleep. Occasionally she would hear Amber move through the apartment, make a coffee in the kitchen, open and close windows, languidly take a call. Charlie would scratch at the door, forcibly headbutt it, yowl. Charlie would shit in his litter box and then, overexcited, arch his back and run across the room, but sideways, in a way that looked like his body shouldn't move, like a crab's or something poorly and disturbingly computer-generated.

Eventually he would settle onto the bed, or in his secret place beneath the bed, groom himself, then slowly fall asleep too. His paw would twitch. Charlie dreamed. Emma did no work.

On the Thursday of her class, Emma bathed, did her make-up to look like she was not wearing make-up and used a steam iron on her clothes. The students in the Digital Arts program didn't dress fashionably. Emma had studied Fine Arts at Parsons and worked nights as a server. Her cohort had smoked cigarettes and dressed like extras in *The Baader Meinhof Complex*. Her students lived on campus. If they smoked, they did so in predesignated areas. They wore sweatpants. To teach, Emma wore clothes she might wear to a client meeting: monochrome, black. As she left the apartment, knowing Amber was out, she let Charlie roam.

On the train she noticed cat hair on her skirt. Then her top. Because Charlie was black she hadn't noticed it in the apartment. It was a lot of hair—all she could see was the hair, but she had already taken the LIRR into Jamaica Station.

At her transfer she thought she could leave the platform and buy a lint roller. Then she realised she didn't know where she would buy a lint roller—a bodega maybe—or what she would do if she left the station, ran to a bodega and a lint roller wasn't there, wasn't available. Emma caught her connection.

Emma stood at the front of the studio class. She tried to stand away from her students so that the students wouldn't notice the hair. They worked on their projects. Sometimes her students spoke to her. Sometimes she used the term 'post-internet'. She would say something vague, like, 'Very post-internet.'

Emma stood behind a student and looked at their screen. A 3D modelling program was open. Maya. Space delineated by a floating grid.

At the end of the semester this student would stand in front of a panel and the panel would be unimpressed. The studio projects were to be more conceptual and ambitious than the ones students would most likely work on professionally, tedious things like what Emma did now. But that was what a lot of students did the course for. The move into industry.

She asked the student what they were trying to do. The student spoke. A lot of student work could be bad. Emma knew this. This was worse.

Emma said, 'Re-evaluate,' and walked away. Emma kept moving.

In her office hour she researched cat behavioural specialists and checked a website on which students rated their college professors like Amazon products. Emma had no new reviews.

When she got home, Dan wasn't there and Charlie was outside Amber's room. He was growling at the door.

Emma had read online that to stop an aggressive cat you should distract it by squirting the cat with water. So that's what she did. She picked up the spray bottle Dan used for their indoor plants. She squirted Charlie. Charlie turned his head towards her and bared his teeth. She squirted again. Charlie chased Emma until Emma herself was stuck in the bathroom, where she stayed for half an hour.

Later, in bed, Emma told Dan that he was meant to have been back from work by the time she got home. He said, 'I went to get Jamaican,' and she hissed, 'Is this serious to you?' He said, 'Yes.'

That weekend they called the specialist in Houston. The specialist asked them to document any 'problem behaviour', including the exact date and time and what Charlie—and any other occupants of the apartment—had been doing in the half hour prior. The specialist recommended that they buy a special spray that mimicked calming cat pheromones.

Emma did this. She bought it the next morning, same day delivery, from Amazon Prime. When Amber was out Emma entered her room and sprayed it on her things. She opened her drawers and sprayed it onto the clothes, the bed, the inside of the closet.

It made no difference.

They logged incidents and did a series of exercises the specialist had emailed them. They had Amber feed Charlie and then they ran through scenarios where Amber walked past Charlie and when Charlie didn't react they gave him a treat. Then they would stop the exercises and say, 'That went great,' and then later Amber would walk to the bathroom to shower and Charlie would jump up and run to the bathroom and hiss at the door. Carefully they would turn up the volume of the television then cover the cat in a large blanket and herd him, still hissing, into their room.

In the dark of their room, on their bed, Dan began to kiss Emma. He pushed his body into hers, and, rolling over, she kissed him back, then said, 'Maybe if we put Charlie's blanket in—' and he said, 'I'm not talking about the cat right now,' and moved away. They lay still on the bed. Charlie began to quietly knead the comforter.

Emma's eyes were open. She saw the pale light of Dan's phone. He set his alarm then made the screen sleep. Neither of them spoke.

On Sunday, Dan cooked French omelettes in a pan they owned solely for the making of French omelettes and juiced organic oranges he'd bought from the farmers' market at Fort Greene Park. They ate, lounging in the living room, paging through art books. Charlie napped in dappled sunlight on the couch, then the desk, the floor.

Looking at the books, Emma experienced a feeling of possibility, that kind of pre-migraine aura she felt before she might make something. The feeling narrowed, then was gone. Emma began to mark her students' studio diaries. She read slowly, holding a red pen. She began to write a note on a paper, then paused. It was hard to focus.

Her thoughts, which first were about her students, began to congregate around Amber, who had gone out the night before and not yet returned but could return at any moment. Emma had begun to dislike Amber. Emma understood that this wasn't fair but disliked her anyway. Amber went to parties in industrial lots and to restaurants that were secretly clubs. Emma thought that Amber thought she was cool, too cool, cooler than Emma, cooler than Dan. Emma didn't think Amber was better than anyone. Amber used ClassPass.

Emma hoped Amber left for spring break. It was almost spring break. Dan asked what Emma wanted to do. There was a family event, on Dan's side, in Tucson. There was going to be a party, a schedule of events. The party had been moved a week to accommodate them—to accommodate Emma's teaching schedule. Dan would meet his latest niece. Emma would be referred to as Auntie Emma. This would not be by the niece, for the niece was a baby and still preverbal, but by Dan's parents and sister.

Emma didn't give a shit about a baby. Emma did not want to go to Arizona. They couldn't take Charlie to Arizona. There wouldn't be anywhere for him to stay and they couldn't leave him at home like they had in the past.

'We can use a cattery,' Dan said. Dan had looked at websites. Dan went through the details, how Charlie would make friends at the cattery, how Charlie would stay in Brooklyn in a 'cat condo'—his own cat-sized studio apartment—how each day the cattery staff took photos of the cats playing in the common area and sent them to their owners. That each day Emma and Dan would wake in Tucson, where it was already warm, and be greeted with a photo or video of Charlie doing Charlie things.

'He'll have a great time,' Dan said.

Emma doubted that the staff took photos of the pets daily. Nothing was to stop them, Emma thought, from taking the photos on admission then meting them out to dumb owners as their cats howled in cages alone. Emma did not say this.

Emma said, 'I don't want to leave Charlie and I have client work to catch up on.'

Dan said, 'But you don't like client work.'

Emma did not like client work but Emma also felt indignant and aggrieved. Emma said, 'This is my career.'

Later, Dan had whispered conversations with his mother, taking a call in their bedroom and then leaving the apartment and talking outside. Amber came home and showered.

A new week began.

In studio, close to the two-hour mark, Emma felt the room's energy dissipate. One group was talking about their plans for spring break. A student in gym shorts had walked in late and was now eating a plate of paella. The student she'd asked to re-evaluate their work had spoken with her and then left the room and not come back. Emma herself was on her laptop responding to client emails. Her clients weren't happy. She had taken too long to do certain things. She had sent the wrong files to the wrong client. She had submitted a render, but in the render a model resident, a woman, was bisected by a concrete wall.

To refocus her students, Emma connected her laptop to the room's projector and told everyone they would watch a video.

The video played through the projector but the audio wouldn't connect to the AV system. The audio only played through the laptop. Emma said, 'This will work if everyone is very quiet.'

They watched the video. It was a YouTube clip about a famous performance artist who had become an architect. In one performance he had placed his entire fist in his mouth, taken it out, then put it back in and violently repeated the gesture. The video showed an assistant seated in front of galvanised metal shelving, describing working at the artist's private firm. The artist's projects weren't always architecture exactly but something closer to art: large-scale installations. His firm lured big commercial clients and then it seemed like the artist would decide he didn't want to do the project and attempt to sabotage it. When the firm would be furiously working towards their deadline, days and nights without sleep, he would stand on a table and yell out lines of poetry and ask the team to express how the poems made them feel. Or he would just yell for them to stop working, then say, 'Maybe we don't want to do this.'

Emma paused the video and opened her mouth to explain the video but nothing came out. Emma felt like her MacBook when it had too many programs open, her brain lagging or about to crash. Her students looked at her. Emma minimised the window and said, 'Okay, now keep going.'

At the end of studio, the students didn't move their chairs back. Emma didn't either.

The next day Emma lured Charlie into the bathroom with a pouch of Fancy Feast and shut the door. She went to campus. She was going to see a student. It was the student who'd left class early. Emma had seen their new work and been honest. The student had circled back, then chosen the same path. Emma told them this. This was all in studio.

The student had requested a meeting. Emma had said, 'My office hours.' The student had said, 'I can't.' Emma had repeated, 'Office hours.' There had been a back-and-forth. Somehow Emma had agreed to meet today, Friday, a day that she did not attend campus. The student had described great emotional turmoil and distress, and Emma had wanted the student to stop talking about great emotional turmoil and distress. She shouldn't have agreed to it. No matter how Emma calculated it, the trip would take four hours, none of which could be claimed.

Emma waited at the coffee shop built into the side of the design building. She sat outside on a small metal bench and emptied her mind. She picked at bits of cat hair on her sweater, looked out at an empty lawn. The student was late. Emma waited. Emma finished one coffee then ordered another. She looked at her staff emails. Five minutes before the meeting time the student had emailed: 'Let's raincheck and try after the break.'

Emma swallowed her coffee. Emma sent an email back. It was strongly worded. Then she sent a few more.

Passing through the woods on the shuttle bus, and then on the train home, first above ground then below, Emma imagined Charlie attacking the student. She imagined this set to tense electronic music.

While she was out, Dan had left early for Tucson, alone.

Spring break started. Charlie's behaviour worsened. It didn't matter what Emma did, whether she did what the specialist told her to do or what the specialist explicitly told her not to do, or whatever the internet prescribed.

Sometimes Emma thought about the cat and then the word 'biblical' in quick succession.

Moving from one room to another room, sitting at her desk, getting up from the desk, going to the bathroom, herding the cat into the bedroom, staying in the bedroom, lying on the bed, getting up from the bed, eating, going to the college or not going to the college but thinking vaguely of the college, Emma had begun to see herself as a model in one of her renders, or more so as an Emma avatar in the game *The Sims* or a *Sims* Brooklyn expansion pack. Emma's avatar was a Sim that was playing *The Sims* to earn money, but that money was only ever enough to keep playing, and, at certain times, upgrade homewares.

The thought of this made Emma want to bare her teeth, to crawl beneath the bed, to roll naked on the floor.

As Emma thought this, Amber had friends over. They wanted to meet the cat. They thought it was funny. Amber was trying to say it wasn't funny but when Amber said it wasn't funny she also laughed. Emma understood they were high. They were in the living room. This was at 2 a.m. Emma could hear them. Emma was working, lying in bed in an oversized t-shirt with her MacBook propped on its side. Charlie came out from under the bed then cocked his head at the door.

Emma thought, Someone is going to knock on my door, and then, There's no way someone would knock on the door.

There was a knock.

Emma lay very still. The MacBook was making an ambient and sustained whirring noise. It was hot to touch. There was another knock. Emma got up and opened the door. A man stood there. He had a pair of piercings on his lower lip, snakebites, and wore a tank top. The year '1998' was tattooed across his Adam's apple.

He said, 'Can we play with the cat?'

Behind him Emma could see Amber and two other girls in the living room sitting on Emma and Dan's couch. Another girl was vaping, sitting at Emma's desk. She opened her mouth and a stream of vapour curled into the air then hung, like a cloud, close to the ceiling.

Emma felt Charlie brush past her legs. The man bent down to the cat and said, 'This guy.'

Charlie looked up at him, quizzically. Then Charlie bit him. Hard. There was movement. Amber was behind the couch and Charlie wouldn't let go of the man's hand. Charlie was exerting pressure. 1998 began to scream. Charlie let go.

Emma picked Charlie up, the cat now writhing, and walked backwards into her room.

Emma went for a drink with a friend. She was a video artist who also worked at a gallery in Bushwick. They went to a bar near Emma's apartment off DeKalb Avenue. The beer garden was still closed for winter though it was spring, so they sat at a table next to a tinted window. Silhouettes passed them on the street.

Emma had left the house because Amber had. Amber had said she was going to a Chinese restaurant that was also a club. Emma googled the club, then thought that as the club was in Manhattan she would have time to have a drink and still get back to the apartment before Amber did.

Emma talked about the situation. Emma said, 'I don't understand why she doesn't just leave.'

'I guess,' Emma's friend said, 'it's really hard to find a place to live here.'

They were drinking white wine. Emma drained a glass and asked the server, 'Is this natural?' and then, 'Don't worry, it's fine.'

Emma's friend spoke about a video work she was developing and then mostly about her life. There was a man, an artist, who would sext her but never follow through. He emailed constantly, then fell silent for days or weeks whenever she tried to take things offline. The man lived in Philadelphia. Emma's friend was thinking of catching a bus to Philadelphia, the 'dick bus' to Philadelphia, though she didn't know exactly where the man lived. She would just go. 'I'll message I'm in Philadelphia and see what happens.'

Emma replied, 'I mean, really, she should move out.'

Emma's friend frowned, then said, 'I guess.'

Emma ordered more wine. She had been in the bar for more than two hours. Emma wanted to go to a party, even a shitty gallery opening, where she could maybe do cocaine. Emma left the bar. Walking home, Emma thought, I still have time, and went into a bodega where she bought Camel Crush Menthols. On the street she lit one and crushed the filter.

Emma stumbled up her apartment stairs. She was intoxicated. She fell. Emma saw herself as if she was looking at herself on her MacBook's screen: a cutaway render of the apartment building and in the stairwell a woman sprawled on the stairs. Emma thought, I'm a drunk, dumb bitch Sim. Emma laughed. Then she stopped laughing. She felt sober, or slightly more sober. She picked herself up and kept climbing.

Amber wasn't home. It was midnight. Emma didn't want to go to sleep so she smoked, half-crouching, half-sitting on the kitchen bench, the window cracked open. She exhaled out the gap. From somewhere she could hear sirens. Charlie moved around the apartment invisible in the dark.

Emma sat there for most of the night.

The next morning Emma lied and told Amber that their lease was over. That the landlord had terminated it without warning. Emma used the term 'unjust'. 'It's unjust,' Emma said, then went to the bodega and the health food store and returned with boxes. She began to put her and Dan's shit in boxes, because that's what it all was. Their art, the kitchen appliances, the cutlery. She stacked one couch on top of the other couch, cleared the living room and began on her bedroom. The more she cleared the more she preferred the apartment that way, empty. Charlie flattened himself inside a box and peeked out.

When Emma took Dan's calls she would say, 'Nothing to report here' and quickly get off the phone. Emma didn't mention their roommate leaving. It was Emma's big win, her big surprise.

Amber had a friend come over to help her move. Emma stayed in the bedroom, the door locked, Charlie asleep under the bed. And then Amber was gone. Emma opened the door. She took a few things out of boxes, then decided she didn't want to take things out of their boxes.

Emma wanted to celebrate. She left the apartment and walked. She was hungry. She stopped in front of a Jamaican restaurant.

When Emma had still made art, whenever she found out a piece would be exhibited, whenever she'd been admitted into a show, she would get drunk, then order vast quantities of food and then eat that food in her studio, lying on her side. Emma went into the restaurant and ordered macaroni and cheese, jerk chicken, cornbread, oxtail, plantains.

Emma made small talk while she waited for her order. She said, 'What a day.' The hostess looked at her then back at her magazine. Emma went outside and smoked a Camel. Through the glass she could see the cooks working in the kitchen. There was a lot going on.

Emma crossed the street. She went into Ideal Food Mart and bought her ideal items: beer, more beer, and high-end cat food to treat Charlie. She crossed back to the restaurant. Her food was ready, waiting for her in a white plastic bag. Emma felt decadent and depraved.

She lit a second Camel as she walked back to the apartment. She arrived at her building with half the Camel left. Emma stood on the landing and held the bag up, the cat food, then the cigarette. Emma decided to finish the cigarette.

Inside, Emma spread the food containers on the bed. She left the bedroom to set out the cat food. As she did this she looked at her phone. There was an email from Google. Whenever Emma's full name was published online, Emma received a Google Alert. She had set this up at a time when certain online magazines wrote about her body of work. This new alert was from ratemyprofessor.com. Emma had a new review from the student she was supposed to meet. The student had uploaded links to screencaps of Emma's emails and had written text below. Scanning, Emma read the words 'abusive' and 'formal complaint'. She put her phone down.

Emma came back to her room. Charlie was on the bed. Charlie was eating the jerk chicken. He had somehow opened the container. She went to touch Charlie but Charlie didn't want to be touched. He jumped off the bed, a piece of chicken breast in his mouth, and went to his secret place beneath the bed. Charlie ate the chicken in his secret place. Emma lay down and picked at the chicken. She ate some mac and cheese. She drank beer. She felt good things, something big inside of her, something triumphant and free.

Charlie came back onto the bed. He sniffed the mac and cheese. He stood beside her, then vomited on the comforter. Emma looked at Charlie and Charlie looked at Emma. There was vomit around his mouth. Emma tried to wipe it. Charlie made a series of rapid noises, then he ran. Emma chased after him through the empty kitchen and the empty bathroom. She cornered him in the living room, her eyes wide, her breath short.

Charlie began to purr.

The Fame

On Grindr I told people I was breaking into the business, but that I was also waiting for the right time. I was a triple threat—a dancer, singer, actor—and then some. I had it, and it was going to make me famous. I just didn't know exactly when or how.

At the time I was living on the Gold Coast. It felt kind of like California, with theme parks, palm trees and water, but it wasn't California. I didn't have the money for a plane ticket to California but it didn't matter. I still sensed a kind of glamour, a feeling that my dreams were not only possible but imminent, that all I had to do was reach out and take them.

I'd come to the Gold Coast following a lead to go-go dance in a nightclub, but when I arrived there was a 'For Lease' sign propped against the club's blacked-out windows. I'd never booked a return flight.

I took a room in a small house, really a bungalow, with two sisters in their late twenties who were both lesbians and matronly. I hadn't needed to pay bond; my room could only fit one single-size mattress on the floor. The yard was all tall grass and weeds, and the front porch had rotted; in the corner was a hole I'd once seen a snake slide into. It lifted its brown head at me, just for a moment, then continued on.

The house was always humid—everywhere was always humid—and mould grew in small constellations across the bathroom ceiling. The sisters worked during the day, carpooling together in the morning. They were something like secretaries. At night they cooked their lunches for the next day and sat in the living room, smoking and watching Foxtel marathons of *Medium*.

I didn't do anything during the day. I didn't practise or prepare. Mainly I massaged the sisters' concealer into the bags under my eyes and streamed episodes of *TMZ* and *E! Entertainment* on my laptop. My favourites were the retrospectives where they showed you where a star came from and then where they came to be. I loved it when they interviewed old friends, classmates. 'Yes, we always knew,' I imagined the sisters in their shitty house repeating on camera.

After a morning of *E!* I walked around the house taking photos of myself. I took hundreds in different light, my head angled a slightly different way, my body posed, my chest topless, my chest not topless. Sometimes I put them on Instagram and dating apps, not because I was looking for sex but because I liked being complimented.

No one ever said it aloud but my body was not the body of a go-go dancer. I didn't exercise, or really eat either. My nipples were weird, kind of far off to the side. I was slim, yes, but my stomach was doughy like a small child's.

When the sun was out I'd take a bus to the beach and walk around the strip of skyscrapers that lined the coast. Then I'd walk down to the sand and pour Diet Coke on myself. I'd read that the artificial sweetener helped to get an even tan.

I did things like that then: take the internet at its word. I lay down on the sand, ants crawling over my chest, and basked in the light till the skyscrapers' shadows lengthened to meet the water and the Hummer limousines came out, ferrying groups of bridal parties from one hotel to another.

My phone sometimes buzzed with apps or my mother's name flashing across my screen. I'd let it ring out. I didn't have time for any of it.

I was eighteen—I'm not much older now—and I truly believed I would be known.

The woman I dealt with at the unemployment agency didn't think what I did classified as work, but she didn't know anything. She'd call me and I'd make excuses for why I couldn't come in.

'You don't really know anything about the entertainment business,' I said. 'It's completely different. I have things lined up. This is a waste of time.'

'If they pay you then you'll need to report that as income.' She always sounded as if she had a cold. 'I can see you've got some missed attendance.'

To collect benefits I had to enrol in a hospitality course, but that took up only one day every two weeks. Then there were modules I had to complete online, but they were the kind of thing where if you clicked the wrong answer they would tell you and you got to pick again.

The other students were all eager. They wanted to do the course five days a week, finish in half a month and work out on the strip. I was happy it stretched out. It was like home economics class except we also learned about alcohol, what drink went into what glass, how to make a highball, a mint julep. We got to taste them at the end of the class, though I never touched my own. I didn't want to drink drinks that I had made, I wanted the world to give them to me. You know, VIP.

I told the woman at the unemployment agency that everything was fine.

'You've got to work with me. You need to do something.'

I did do something. At night I went to Cabana, a karaoke bar next to the casino. It had a tiki theme. Drinks came in deep totem mugs, chunks of pineapple skewered on cocktail umbrellas. There was a water feature by the bar. It was kitsch, tacky if you know what I mean, but it was close to the one recording studio I could find on Google and I figured agents or producers might hang out there.

It always took me hours to get ready, to do my hair, de-lint my clothes, although I always wore the same thing. I'd sit in the corner of the bar in my sunglasses and my gold sequined woman's bolero, then walk to the stage, pick up a ticket and wait. I tried to go on at a specific time, eleven-fifteen. It made me feel like I was a lounge singer, a regular, someone to be discovered.

Things like that happen. People don't think they do, but they can. It's on *E!*. This star did it, this one too, it's all towards something. Every star has a story they tell once they're famous about when they weren't. I spent a lot of time just thinking how I was writing my own.

When my song came on I'd step onto the podium, my bolero flaring in front of the silver drapes, stare out at the crowd and sing. I was happy to sing. It gave me pleasure and in turn I gave it a lot. I had moves, my own choreography, and looking out I'd feel giddy because I had a secret, and it was that one day they would all be paying to see the show.

I'd do two songs and when my set was over I'd tell everyone my name then go back to my corner and drink soda water till closing time when a man with a gut began wiping the tables and stacking the chairs. Night after night no one ever spoke to me.

I liked it. I felt that was how it was meant to be.

One Friday as I was dressing to go out the sisters came home from their work Christmas parties. The older one was wearing a Santa hat. They were drunk and barged into the bathroom as I was using their cosmetics. They didn't say anything about it, they just wanted to know where I was going. I was coy but finally I told them and they begged to come with me. They said they'd pay for a taxi, that we could all take it. I said I was fine with the bus.

'We'll be your entourage,' one said. The two of them looked at each other. I had to think about it. I said yes.

We waited in the kitchen for the taxi, and I remember the sisters sitting at the linoleum table, ashing their cigarettes into an oversized Movie World mug. The sun had set hours ago but outside it was still hot and the sky faintly glowed the way it does in summer. I stood in front of the fan and looked out the window at the palms and the lone streetlight.

We got to the bar and they ordered drinks. One ate the other's pineapple chunk. I can't say which—it was difficult to distinguish the two of them, because I wasn't interested in them or their lives. Looking back, it's hard to say why I disliked them so much. Sometimes they let me pay rent late. I think it was just that their lives were ordinary. They were everything I despised and feared.

'When's your slot?' the one with the Santa hat asked.

The other, 'Do you have fans? Are there regulars?'

They were making fun of me but I was very earnest at the time.

The sisters sang 'Cruisin'' from *Duets*, the one with Gwyneth, and then I got up and did a number. Halfway through, one of them fell off her stool. A tiki mug rolled across the floor and a bouncer approached them and asked them to leave. I kept singing.

I sat down with my soda water and found that somehow I missed them. I spent a lot of time alone watching other people be around other people. I watched the stage. A couple sang the song from *Aladdin* about a whole new world, an Asian woman whispered 'Time after Time', a fat man in a Hawaiian shirt sang Cher. They were all ugly, their choices uninspired, the deliveries all derivative.

Close to one o'clock the stage was empty. The couple who sang *Aladdin* were in a booth. The girl sat on top of the guy and he put his hands up her skirt and she giggled, brushing them off, then placed them back. My phone vibrated with a notification. It was Grindr.

The man was thirty-six and his profile photo showed a sunset on a beach. The message read, 'ur voice is very beautiful.'

I played it cool, not looking around. I just watched the couple. My phone vibrated again.

'I work in music.'

My heart leapt. I replied, 'Tell me more.'

———

After that night the bar started charging a cover fee. It was only fifteen dollars but it was a lot for me. My benefits weren't high. At first I tried to walk in like I worked there, but every time the bouncer, who resembled more than anything a *TMZ* cameraman, stood in my way and held out his hand.

At home, when I did eat I boiled rice and then to flavour it I skimmed from whatever the sisters had put in Tupperware for the next day. I was beginning to get nervous that I would have to leave the Gold Coast before I was discovered. That I would return home to my mother's, to a shitty suburb in Adelaide, and go back to working at the pharmacy handing out samples of celebrity fragrances that weren't my own.

My life in Adelaide wasn't bad, but like the sisters' it was ordinary. My mother took medication for a botched operation that was meant to put in a gastric band. I had no brothers, no sisters. I was all she had. The last time I saw my father he'd shown me a building in Edwardstown where you could collect food stamps. On the Gold Coast I told people I was an orphan.

I had high hopes for my Grindr messenger. He'd told me—or at least I was sure—that he had connections, but I had to wait for him to put those connections into play. 'send more pics,' he messaged. And I did. I had the sisters take my headshots and then some photos of me posed topless on my bed—selfies seemed unprofessional. The sisters agreed.

He sent me a photo of himself. He looked cool, like he could be in a magazine. He was wearing a leather jacket and sunglasses. He looked like Kevin Bacon.

Sometimes I looked at his profile picture and tried to guess where it had been taken. The sunset didn't seem to be the kind you could see here—the sun was setting over the water, so the water was to the west. I thought maybe it was the same Pacific I looked out at, but from the other side.

I still wanted to go-go dance. I thought that, now that my career was in motion, I had to be more forward-thinking. I felt karaoke in a tacky bar was better than karaoke in just any bar, but it wasn't enough. It wouldn't justify an *E!* special that could last an episode, let alone a miniseries. It also didn't pay.

I went back to the closed nightclub on the same bus I took to the bar. The lead I had got to come to the Gold Coast was from months earlier, from a drag queen named Madame Chiffon. She had performed in a bar in Adelaide with a troupe of barely clad men. Drinking from a jug of beer, she told me to come to her club and audition. After the show, the dancers moved around the bar and were given free drinks.

I thought about that night a lot then. How people took photos of themselves with the dancers and how I watched a woman in her forties try to tug at the elastic of one of their thongs. It wasn't fame but it was something that could tide one over.

This time, when I arrived, the club's windows weren't blacked out and I could see inside. There was empty space, sawdust and labourers. I asked one as they came outside what was happening. He wore an orange vest and said the space was being turned into apartments. I asked the workers if they knew Madame Chiffon. They looked at me, told me to get lost, that they weren't fags. I told them to fuck themselves. I walked a little down the road and sat on the footpath. I did what I always did then: I focused and visualised myself surrounded in bright, flashing light.

A week later at the learning centre I sat at a chipboard table and role-played being a customer. I had put my hand up when the instructor asked for a volunteer. I'd done drama at school.

I sat at the table and asked, 'How do you want me to say the line?'

'It doesn't matter.'

A student walked over to me. He had red hair, a septum piercing and wore a Kmart t-shirt. He had no style. He handed me a piece of paper—my menu—and mimed filling a glass with water. He asked, 'What can I get you?'

I said what I wanted, but left it slightly unclear with my delivery because I figured most people don't know what they want, and when they do they're not bold enough to get it. I really opened up the scene. The redhead just stood there.

'What was that?' the instructor said.

'I improvised.'

The instructor looked at me. 'Just ask if the sandwich can be gluten-free. That's it.'

We went again. The instructor asked for someone else to take my spot.

At home, as I lint-rolled my bolero, I thought, I don't need any of this. I messaged my messenger. 'Do you think I could be on TV? At some point I want to do TV.'

He said, 'yes. we make video.'

I saw the benefits. A show reel.

———

After that I stopped going to my classes, stopped signing in online. It was too much. It made me self-reflexive. It took me to a bad place. Instead, I went to the beach.

On the bus, passing palm after palm framed in a blue sky, I dreamed of Beverly Hills, Rodeo Drive, Malibu.

When I came home, without looking up from the television the sisters reminded me it was rent week. Then one of them said, 'The internet is going very slow.' It wasn't a statement but an accusation. Then she said, 'There's mail for you,' and pointed to the bench. It was from the employment agency. The humidity had already made the envelope damp. I didn't open it. I walked outside and dropped it in the porch's hole. It was their third letter. They all sat together in the dark. I came back inside.

Lying on my mattress, sweating, I tried to stream an interview with a singer who had once cleaned the houses of record producers and left copies of her demo tapes in their stereos. The internet was slow. The singer stuttered. 'You . . . have . . . to re-ally . . . wa-nt . . . it.' I shut the laptop and lay in my want. I wanted my messenger to message me and for him to call a black car for me, a limousine with reflective windows that would take me to a dark, sound-proofed room where I would make my future.

When I imagined my future then it was always fame. I didn't question it. It was something that was rushing to meet me, to envelop me, and when it did people would recognise and want to be me. Personal assistants would open and reply to my fan mail. Luxury brands would send me pieces and kiss my feet if I chose to wear them. I would smile, or my eyes would suggest a smile, and that image would be across the covers of tabloid magazines, smartphone backgrounds and projected, a hundred metres high, onto the backdrop of an arena stage.

My phone vibrated. It was him. 'hi.'

I asked if that night he could put me on the list for Cabana. He didn't reply.

Eventually I did meet Madame Chiffon. I had found the club's Facebook page and trawled through their uploaded pictures until I found one of her that was tagged. The page showed that she was a she, and not a man. I sent her a private message. She replied immediately, which I took as a good sign.

I was frustrated because it had been weeks of my messenger messaging me and nothing was happening. I had a growing sense that nothing would happen. I intended to get a new agent, someone who would take me where I needed to be.

I met Madame Chiffon in a food court beneath the CBD. She was already sitting down. I wore a dark mesh singlet and oversized pumps. I wanted to impress. I told her that when we'd first met I'd thought she was a drag queen.

'Oh, I put, like, gel packs in my bra and use a wig. Do my make-up like a clown. The scene doesn't love women.'

She tilted her chin towards her neck and then sort of goggled her eyes. I saw the resemblance, even though she now wore an outfit identical to something the sisters might wear: nylon tights, a plain skirt, a business blouse.

'You told me to come by when I was in town,' I said. 'I was ready to audition.'

She looked at me, really looked at me, and then said, 'Did you look different?'

'You came to Adelaide and did a show.'

'Honey, when I'm dressed up I'm off my tits. The club's shut anyway.'

'So what do you do now?'

'I call people and tell them about insurance packages.'

'Oh.' I held my hands in my lap.

She took a mouthful of Thai food and followed it with a swig of Coke.

'Yeh,' she said. 'My break ends in ten.'

'Are there any places I should try?'

A cleaner came and waited in front of us, then took her plastic plate. I held my breath.

'I don't know.' She got up. 'Maybe start going to a gym.'

Feeling low and stupid, I walked through the city and onto the beach. I held a can of Diet Pepsi to my chest. The city seemed so small. It was sunny but I didn't care.

I sat down and pulled my top off, splashing my shoulders with Diet Pepsi that ran down my chest and stomach in rivulets. A man jogged by with two white balls of muscle, pit bulls, off leash. They bounded towards me and I put my hands up, scared, but all they did was lick at my nipples. The man ran up to them and grabbed them by the scruffs. He wore a blue wife-beater and had a Southern Cross tattoo on one bulging triceps. I put my arms down and he stared at me as if to say, What the hell's the deal with you? I didn't look back. I stayed poised. When the dogs were two white points in the distance I got up and began to walk back to the bungalow.

I stopped outside the strip mall near the house, thinking

to buy a juice—something to elevate my mood. The strip mall was dark, with lots of fake marble stucco and plastic palms. It was the kind of place that sold glow-in-the-dark Buddhas, fake porcelain cats, two-for-one packs of tracksuit pants. There was an Asian grocery store, an accountant's and a beauty parlour. If I wanted juice I'd have to buy it in a carton.

I walked into the parlour. I remembered that a singer I adored had once told a talk-show host that in a dark period of her life, whenever she felt down, she got blazed and had her driver take her to see a woman, 'her girl', who injected her face full of Juvéderm. The singer wasn't even thirty years old.

I asked the woman at the front counter if they did fillers. She was middle-aged and kind of bloated. Looking at my face, she scrunched up her eyes and said, 'Yes,' and then, 'You're very young.'

'I know how to take care of my skin.'

We went to a room in the back that had no windows, just brown carpet. I said I wanted Juvéderm. It gave me a high, just saying those syllables aloud, as if I was saying *lu-xu-ry*, *bo-ttle ser-vice*, *pa-tron*. I sat on a padded chair like at a dentist. The woman put purple latex gloves on, pulled them taut, then left the room and came back in wheeling a tray with syringes. She asked where I wanted it. I pointed to under my eyes. 'My lips too.' She stared at them, gauging them. I liked the attention.

When she told me how much it would cost I pulled out my phone and checked my bank balance. It was low— my payments had been suspended. I said I didn't have enough.

'How much do you have?'

I showed her the screen. She nodded.

'It's not Juvéderm but I could do a bit of something.'

My lips were swollen but I thought they looked good, like Angelina Jolie's. I went home and tried on different outfits, then settled on my bolero, doing a twirl as I put it on. I felt confident. I felt good.

I sent a text to my messenger. I typed, 'Tonight we should meet,' and crept out of my room, taking fifteen dollars from the purse of one of the sisters.

At Cabana I sang but I botched the notes. My lips were numb and the words stuck to each other.

Someone heckled. I got off the stage and went to the bathroom, splashed my face with cold water. I thought the world was awful but that the crowd, all of them, would be on my *E!* special too. I waited in line again to sing. I thought, *E!* special, *E!* special, but when I stood in front of the silver drapes again I didn't do any better.

My phone vibrated. 'yes, we meet.'

I said, 'I'm sorry I botched all the notes.'

'a star isnt notes.'

I asked, 'Am I a star?'

'yes.'

I held the phone to my chest.

It was five-fifteen in the morning. He had sent me his location. He didn't want to meet at the club. He said the club was seedy. Instead we met somewhere worse—his flat, one of many, making an L around a gravel car park like a Holiday Inn. I don't know what I was expecting. A view from a great height, glasses of Cristal.

I stood in front of his door and sent a message: 'here.' I thought about doing scales, warm-ups, but my face was too hot. I stood there and scratched at my cheeks, the skin between my eyebrows and eyes.

The door opened. He didn't look like he did in his pictures because the man in his pictures was someone else. They didn't even have the same haircut. He was middle-aged, his stomach bulging out of his singlet, long cracked toenails visible in sandals. It was the cleaner from the bar. He put a finger to his lips, made a sort of cooing sound then took my arm, leading me into a dark room and closing the door behind me.

It was squalid. The sheets on the bed were dirty. There were crumbs, stains, an overturned glass. It wasn't all that different from where I was living, but there was a dog, the kind you could put in a handbag. It looked like a big rat. It bit at its skin and yapped.

The man looked at me the way the beautician had, up close. He told me I was pretty, then kissed me. He put a hand up my top and ran his fingers over my nipples. He was very gentle. I still wanted to talk about myself, my big career, but he turned me over, placed my face into the mattress, pulling on my hips till I was on my hands and knees. He tucked my underwear down. It felt like my face was on fire and then I felt something wet slide over my arse. It was his tongue. He slid it in.

The dog yapped and yapped and yapped. The man stopped, yelled at it in a language I didn't understand, then brought his tongue back and flicked it around. He moved up, slowly brought his crotch to my arse.

For a while I stared at the sky through the closed curtains, grey slowly washing to pink, the shadow of a palm, then myself in the wardrobe's mirror, kneeling, him panting over me. A red rash had spread down my face and my right eyelid was almost closed over, puffed up like a cyst, a purple balloon. Behind me I saw a webcam propped up on a tripod, its little red light blinking.

For a moment I thought I couldn't breathe but then I remembered how. It wasn't that my face was fucked up or that I was a virgin or anything like that. I wasn't a virgin any more than he was an agent, but for those moments, for the first time, I saw myself and I knew I didn't look like a star. I didn't look like anyone. I looked like no one at all.

That morning I did the only thing I knew how to do: I turned towards the camera and put on a show.

Contact

At her interview, the woman wears a pantsuit and has her hair tied back. It is her third interview to discuss the same position. She sits and leans forward, smiling, her lipstick a professional nude. A panel of four give her a sheet of paper that lists different nouns. They ask which value on the sheet best describes her. She looks at the panel, vaguely eye-level, and lies, saying what she thinks will seem most impressive from a person her age. She says, 'Self-respect.'

There is a young woman, more of a girl, straight out of high school, interviewing with her. The girl hesitates for a moment, then says, 'Empathy.' She just loves people. The woman feels this is a better answer, so she announces that she also knows the NATO phonetic alphabet. The girl replies, 'Alfa. Bravo. Charlie.' They are both hired.

They are walked around the floor and introduced to the fire wardens, are told the number to dial for first aid and what to do if someone calls in and says they have planted a bomb in the building. There is a surprising number of things to do if someone calls in and says there is a bomb in the building, partly because it is a large building.

It was not called a call centre in the job listing or the woman's interview, but after the woman gets the position everyone calls it the call centre because that's exactly what it is.

The call centre is on the seventh floor of a concrete office building. A swipe card gives access to the elevators and the women's bathroom. The centre itself is twenty desks, open plan, with old Cisco telephones, headsets and fluorescent lighting. On her first day she notices a poster on the window behind her supervisor's desk. It says, 'Don't Jump,' but then, after six months, the girl from the interview swipes her swipe card and takes the elevator to the roof. She jumps. The poster is quietly taken down.

The calls are timed. Everything is timed. The time between calls. How long it takes to email responses. How long she takes in the bathroom. The minute she arrives and the minute she leaves. This data is collated into reports and spreadsheets. The data that isn't captured: how frequently the woman imagines someone giving her a large sum of money and expecting little, if anything, in return.

The woman has the job because she doesn't know the type of person she is or wants to be. She knows she is the type of person who prefers to live alone, and the job, because it is with the government or at least is government-adjacent, means she can afford, for the first time, at age thirty-two, to rent an apartment without a flatmate. The apartment is basic and has little light, downtown on the fourteenth floor of a cheaply constructed residential tower. From the elevator to her front door she walks through a nondescript hallway she views as a low-rendered loading screen she must navigate as her apartment buffers. This is also how she views her job.

The job appeals to her in other ways too. It is good, she supposes, to have a job, because she doesn't have the kind of education that leads to any one career, and though the job is not really a career, on the first Wednesday of each month a Chinese man stands in Meeting Room Two and gives her a fifteen-minute shoulder massage.

The work itself she loathes. She answers calls, redirects them or links callers to other services. She clarifies names and addresses, which is difficult because people call in on speakerphone or do not enunciate or consider that an 's' and an 'f' sound identical when spelled over the phone.

Her co-workers seem strange and have odd body types. A woman has a goiter. A man has a medical condition that means he cannot sweat. Another, perioral dermatitis. The woman is unsure whether she is an outlier in the department or of the same type. In her apartment she stands naked in front of the bathroom mirror and surveys what she sees. Slowly, she rotates.

At work she is sent questionnaires that will be tabulated and used selectively to justify operational and organisational change. There are constant restructures, but they happen on higher floors and feel far away, the subjects of company-wide emails the woman leaves unread. The woman does not take time to read her emails and instead frequently gets up from her desk to fill a mug with filtered water. She returns to her desk and joins the call queue. Her headset rings.

A caller barks, 'Are you a computer?'

The woman has been told that she should put more emotion but not too much emotion into greeting customers. The woman believes a finite amount of emotion can be put into the words 'This call is being recorded' and that that finite amount has already been exhausted.

She replies, 'Can I start with your name?'

'I'm the one asking the questions, not the computer.'

The woman thinks about all the things she could say but does not say them. She says, 'Please hold.'

When the woman was younger she wrote poems and lived in a variety of houses and apartments, a sequence of boxes that were rooms: one above an Italian restaurant, another next door to a twenty-four-hour convenience store, a small room with a very high ceiling on the top floor of a crumbling terrace house, and between these, due to an administrative error, a large span of time in student housing when she was no longer technically a student. For money she replied to customer emails for a food delivery service, she delivered food for said food delivery service, she wrote fake Google reviews, and she dressed and undressed people in flowing graduation robes. She did these jobs so she could write. She spent her money on rent, sessions with a psychologist and low-quality party drugs.

Late at night she would write poems with little to no punctuation, with titles like 'streaming deep impact', 'kristen stewart eats a salad', 'bad artist statement', believing they attempted to communicate the incommunicable. Mainly they described the things she or other people had done but in the present tense as if in the moment of doing them.

At certain chemically imbalanced points, on MDMA for instance, she thought the poems were the best poems in the world.

Some people thought they were okay and others hated them. Most people just didn't read poems. And then the woman stopped writing for the same reasons everyone else did: she had to make more money.

Now when the woman has money she spends it and thinks, Cash flow, and when she doesn't, she thinks, I need more money.

There is a work event. The woman intends not to go. She goes. It is at a bar where she must pay for her own drinks. She orders a vodka soda then goes into the bathroom and into a stall. She sits on the toilet and thinks about how long she has to stay at the bar before she can leave, and how much of that time can be spent sitting in the stall sipping her vodka soda. She thinks about what percentage of that time can be spent sipping the same vodka soda before that vodka soda must be replenished.

She goes back to the work group. Then she says aloud, 'I'm just getting a drink.' At the bar, men in suits wave corporate cards. She buys her second vodka soda. She returns to the group but wonders when she can make her way back to the bathroom.

During shifts she rarely speaks to co-workers because she is always speaking on the phone. Here, people are talking.

She discovers that a gay man in her department used to work as a female phone-sex operator. He is a man but his voice is very feminine, and also husky in a way that makes the woman think of late-night movies, French films. Another man is a semi-professional wrestler. A younger woman who often works at the desk next to hers makes artisanal candles and sells them online. 'If I get a distributor,' she says, 'I can finally leave.'

This all disturbs the woman. A feeling that is unspecific yet total hangs over her. She thinks she has nothing to define her outside of her job, and this thought causes her to take a series of quick, shallow breaths. On the tram ride home she looks up the online candle store and then Facebook-stalks the staff member who wrestles. She stalks until she finds photos of the man glistening in oil. She has had four vodka sodas and finds it challenging to read text on her phone. She follows links until, somehow, she is watching a thirty-second video of a javelina galloping through an urban environment, passing a busy intersection and the driveway of an apartment complex, before the video plays again. The javelina does not know where it is running and yet runs. The woman watches the video fourteen times.

The woman is more than slightly drunk. She understands something. She is the javelina.

In the woman's apartment is a small spare bedroom, and in that room a desk. She imagines herself sitting at the desk writing poems again. Then she stops imagining. When she comes home from work she sits at the desk or on her bed and does the same things she does at work—looks at the same websites, refreshes the same pages—but at home, if her phone rings, she does not answer it, and when she streams videos she plays them with sound.

There is a meeting. The meeting is held three times so that there are always people left to staff the phones. In the meeting the employees are flattered. There are free donuts and instant coffee. The department manager tells them that they are all holders of vital intellectual property, and that to better understand that property management have brought in an outside agency that will observe them, then use that property to digitise services, streamlining phone-to-phone experiences to online. The department manager says, 'This is a very exciting time.' The man who cannot sweat asks if they are all losing their jobs. The manager says, 'You guys,' and ends the meeting.

These meetings now take place weekly.

The agency staff wear all-black, ask questions and write the answers on Post-it notes they then attach to the walls, office furniture and other staff members. The agency staff can be seen in different parts of the call centre at different times, crouching behind the woman, rolling down the hallway on silver yoga balls, riding up and down in the elevators sipping from takeaway espresso cups.

The woman doesn't mind the meetings because during them she does not have to answer calls. Mainly she nods. At the end of the meetings she sits back at her desk and refreshes a webpage while calculating her annual leave.

———

At home the woman listens to a podcast which is largely about the ways in which women and small children can and have been murdered. She listens to the podcast and boils store-bought tortellini. When the tortellini are done she does not put sauce on them or butter or cheese—she slices a tomato and alternates between bites of tomato and bites of tortellini which she eats directly from the colander. As she listens, a woman is stabbed, a child suffocated. She thinks of a poem title. A poem's title can give as much satisfaction as a poem. Sometimes more. She hears the description of a sashimi knife and then a message from the podcast's sponsors. She forgets the poem title.

She lies in bed, the podcast still playing, her eyes open in the dark.

A wall is taken out and the break room becomes the breakout space with a long table and high stools. There is also a white-board. The whiteboard is filled with Post-its. The woman eats her lunch, a pre-packaged salad, in the breakout space, unless a meeting has been booked or begins impromptu, in which case she is asked to leave.

The agency staff have been replaced with consultants who also wear black and stand by the whiteboard and move Post-its.

As services turn digital there are fewer hours. Sometimes the woman shows up for work and is asked to go home. Whenever she is asked to go home the woman logs out of the computer and thinks, Yippee.

On her way home, sometimes the woman has sex with a man in her apartment building. He is a copywriter who works from home. The man says, 'I would like to go down on you.'

The woman says, 'I consent.'

Later she will write a poem. The poem will describe the empty Domino's boxes in the copywriter's bedroom and the copywriter weakly ejaculating. As she writes she will feel something close to joy.

One morning, riding the tram, the woman spots her former psychologist. She saw the psychologist for emotional issues that remain unresolved. Her psychologist always wore clothes that were overly large, like Jared in the old Subway commercials.

When she was seeing the psychologist he gave her certain exercises she did not want to do because they seemed like exercises the psychologist would give anyone, exercises that didn't take into account the specifics of her situation, its complexity. When she had a bad thought she was to replace it with a good one. She tried it. If she thought about how depressing her life was, she thought, Hamsters. This seemed to work, though it filled her with shame. She did not relay any of this to the psychologist because, at the time, she had felt that they were locked in a battle of wills.

On the tram her psychologist is wearing a large grey suit. Her psychologist sees her, he is looking at her, then he closes his eyes and freezes like she is a T-rex and if he doesn't move she will not see him.

She thinks, My psychologist thinks I am a T-rex. Later, at home, she thinks, I have an exciting and vivid inner life.

There is a problem: the woman has significantly fewer hours. She speaks to her manager. She says, 'But I'm permanent.' And they reply, repeating the word 'flexible'.

Because the woman is working less she can no longer afford to live in the apartment alone. She moves the desk into her room and advertises the second bedroom. Men message her questions about square footage, and one does not ask about the apartment but says he will only live with the woman if she has pretty little feet. She rents the room to a thirty-year-old homosexual because no women have messaged her and she believes homosexuals are naturally neat.

On the day her flatmate moves in he plays very loud house music and throws a party. Her online listing stated 'No parties'. At the party, men wear leather harnesses. There is a large amount of bare skin. People unscrew bottles of amyl nitrite and sniff.

The woman turns on the kitchenette grill's fan.

She says, 'This is a party.'

Her flatmate says, 'I don't think it is.'

The website on which the woman used to publish her poems is no longer popular. This is because the site banned porn. Most people used the site for porn, even the woman, and sometimes when people looked at porn, they also looked at poems. The porn on the site could be quite artful and the poems explicit.

Instead of posting a new poem on the site she sends the poem to an old friend. The friend released two chapbooks and used to give readings where she would stand on the counter at a bar, her entire body wrapped in aluminium foil, a small tear at her mouth. The friend replies that she no longer reads or writes poetry. The friend replies that she cares about the real world. The friend replies, 'Who needs chapbooks.' The friend replies, 'AI writes poetry.'

The woman does not respond.

Even when the friend and the woman were friends, the woman thinks, they were not very good ones.

The woman no longer receives Chinese massages, but the consultants do. They come out of the conference room and roll their shoulders. They say, 'You really have to try this.'

She puts a customer on hold and forgets she has put the customer on hold, and goes to the bathroom. She crouches in a toilet stall and feels something amorphous and urgent and dull.

She comes back to her desk. There is a small red light blinking on the woman's phone. The customer is still on hold. The woman was in the bathroom for an extended period of time and cannot remember what the customer wants, only that they want something. She answers the call as if it is a new one.

Later a man repeats the words, 'I've had enough! I've had enough!' But she doesn't know what exactly he has had and what about it is enough, only that he can speak for thirty-six minutes, breathless, and at the end of that thirty-six minutes hiss, 'You are a cunt.'

The time between calls is cut from five seconds to three. In three-second intervals the woman reads articles titled 'Ways to Enrich Your Life', 'You Are Navigating Your Time on this Earth Inefficiently', 'It Is OK to Cry in Bathroom Stalls But Only When Alone'. She reads that it is nice to do something communal in a shared household, something to break the ice.

She thinks drinking wine is sophisticated. She thinks, I am a sophisticated woman. She texts her flatmate to say that after work they should have a drink. He replies many hours later, 'Okay.'

She waits at home. She thinks, Maybe he is at the gym. She waits some more. She eats the wheel of brie she has put out. Then she eats the crackers. Then, the grapes. She starts on the grapes' stem. It is 1 a.m.

The flatmate returns from the gym.

He says, 'I was going to leave you a note.' He is holding the note. He reads it aloud. 'I would prefer if we lived separate but cohabited lives. I am not comfortable with social interactions with a stranger and cannot help you or your problems.'

The woman slurs, 'That is reasonable.'

She has drunk three bottles of rosé.

The woman is called into the conference room for a meeting. The meeting is to go over the woman's stats. The stats will be on a computer screen in the form of a large and complex Excel spreadsheet. The woman walks to the conference room and thinks, I'm fucked, I'm fucked.

In the conference room they go over the statistics. Her manager pats her back. The woman's stats are better than they've ever been. This makes little sense. The woman does not say this. She says, 'I'm just doing my job,' and quickly retreats from the conference room.

Sometimes, sitting in the call centre, the woman feels like she is balanced upon a high ledge, and what the ledge tumbles down to is unknown to her, inarticulable. And sometimes she doesn't feel like she is on the ledge but that she is already falling, and when she does her vision seizes and the double monitor in front of her blurs. Then it passes. This is not unusual.

Like changing tabs. An image. A GIF. A closed-circuit loop.

There are men in her apartment. They are shirtless and make cosmopolitans. No one acknowledges her. Her flatmate is in the centre of the living room, his body oiled, lounging on her couch, in nothing except a lime-green thong. He holds a bottle of amyl. He opens it and sniffs. She goes directly to her room.

Some workers move to other departments. The woman requests to be transferred but the request is denied. She thinks, Hamsters, then, Ha ha ha.

———

Because the online service is confusing and sometimes a customer will follow a link and the link will be broken, or the link will take them to strange places—a livestream from the International Space Station, a page for purchasing opera tickets somewhere in Eastern Europe, archives of unredacted FOI documents—people still call the centre. This is a point of resentment among the consultants.

When they pass the woman they spit on the carpet. It is unclear who the consultants are still consulting.

The woman answers the phone. Customers speak in tongues.

The man who was formerly a phone-sex operator changes roles. Every now and then the woman hears his voice, husky, projected through a PA system the woman cannot see. Announcements begin with, 'This may or may not be a drill.' A month passes, then another and another. The woman hears, 'There is a fire in the building and fires outside the building.' She hears, 'Do not touch surfaces. Where possible, minimise breathing.' She hears, 'There are terrorists in the building. We believe they are crawling through the ventilation system.' There is the sound of explosions, and then the phone-sex operator's voice. 'Yippee ki-yay, motherfuckers.'

She works on poems again, little stabs at the infinite. Sometimes she sits on her bed with a poem in front of her, and other times, when her flatmate is out, she goes into his room, opens his bedside drawer, and takes out his bottle of amyl.

She unscrews the top and sniffs, one nostril, then the other. For a moment the borders of herself become diffuse, permeable, each colour more intense, the flickering of something vast and endless, a great, bright light, but then the doors to perception close and she goes back and sits in her room.

The consultants believe the office is over. Cubicles. Open plan. All of it. The consultants announce this and rapturously applaud. The woman now works from home, sitting cross-legged on her bed. Sometimes she is beneath the covers, sometimes above. Incoming calls flash across the screen of her phone. She opens her mouth and closes it. Her flatmate slips Post-its under her door. The Post-its read, 'You have a very irritating voice.'

In this way things continue but are slightly worse. People call, afraid, and ask the big questions. Life. Death. The possibility of quantifiable proof of the human soul.

The woman has recurring dreams. In most of them she is working, but in one the woman holds a money gun that spits out hundred-dollar bills. The woman dances like she is in a music video. She aims the gun in the air and shoots.

An MFA Story

The summer before the summer I was meant to graduate from graduate school I had a short story collection to put together and one hundred dollars left of my stipend. I'd not been awarded a teaching fellowship, which would've paid me to teach 'advanced' high school students short fiction over the break, and my F-1 visa meant I could not be employed outside of the university or I could face immediate deportation.

I explained my situation to others. In the last week of workshop, my friend Lydia and I went to our local dive bar that had no windows, smelt like sweat and wouldn't allow people in if they wore backwards-facing caps. We were day-drinking and Lydia was deciding which books she would take with her when she left for the break. A gay couple her mother knew had a house in Maine. They were travelling and didn't want the house to be broken into by teenage drunks. Lydia would house-sit. She knew my predicament but did not invite me. I asked her anyway. She said no.

This reluctance characterised most people I knew: writers and poets who were taking Greyhounds south and either sunbathing in Williamsburg or waiting tables in their hometowns where they didn't need to pay rent. Lydia would take the summer to write three stories, one per month, and luxuriate sleeping naked atop strangers' sheets.

With another three stories, at least as full drafts, we would each have a collection, the rough object of our master's theses due in seven months' time.

We made a pact to spend our summers writing, and hugged each other outside the bar. The sky turned gold with the slow beginnings of dusk.

I was being paid to be in graduate school but only for the months graduate school was in session. I was lucky. My position was fully funded, student debt would not bury me and professors on the program's faculty had appeared on *The Late Show with Stephen Colbert*. Only five fiction writers and five poets were admitted to the program each year. I wasn't an American national. I had applied from Melbourne, FedExed a stack of fiction along with my personal statement, my letters of recommendation. I got in and it was a big deal.

When I found out, I burnt bridges. I told my boyfriend who I thought was holding me back that he was holding me back and that he wouldn't hold me back, or really hold me at all, anymore. I said similar things to my family. I boarded a flight, flew over an ocean and read through a seven-hour layover in Dallas. Then I arrived in the city and realised from my taxi driver's monologue and the number of boarded-up storefronts that the city was in a decades-long depression. People were routinely assaulted, the population was heavily armed and New York State was in fact very, very far from New York City.

The workshop was challenging. Though my application had said I viewed criticism as an avenue for growth, this was a lenient version of the truth. I had lied but only about the things everyone lies about. When criticised I first resent the speaker and then, afterwards, writhe sunken and alone on my bedroom floor.

But I was fine. I was not the worst in the class, nor was I the best, which didn't worry me. I knew that a writer could be defined by their potential work—that is, even at twenty-nine, the work I hadn't yet done.

My contemporaries dealt with the stress of the workshop in different ways. A man lifted stories of muggings, forced evictions and suspicious property fires from the local paper and said he was writing the first great novel of the opioid crisis. When a book came out that winter that was hailed as 'the first great novel of the opioid crisis', he stopped coming to workshop. One woman baked elaborate things she brought into class, ensuring, I believe, that the feedback on her novel was gentler and more kind. Another woman rarely shared work, had possibly stopped writing, but cultivated a Twitter following of seven thousand and would underline sentences in people's work she found problematic and then tweet those sentences to her followers. There were complaints to the faculty. The administration did not want to be tweeted about by those seven thousand followers and so stayed out of it altogether.

Now, with a hundred dollars—well, after the bar, seventy dollars—I walked home, avoiding crossing directly through the darkening park, and thought about the months ahead.

I didn't have the money for a ticket to Melbourne. Even if I had I feared that if I went back to Australia I would not come back here, that something would detain me: money, immigration officials, a realisation or epiphany. Instead I would spend the three months here living with my house-mate, Zhen, a poet from China who often wore slide-on sandals with gym socks. Zhen had had work published in *The Paris Review* and *Harper's* and so had been the subject of faculty-wide emails with photos of him sheepishly smiling, the journals held up under his chin. His poems were every-thing I wanted my stories to be. Beautiful. Surprising. Alive.

Our flat was actually the second storey of an old Victorian the owner had converted into a duplex. A rickety wooden staircase attached to the house's side led to our dead-locked front door. Zhen and I lived there together for one reason: we were both foreign. Two years ago the program secretary had cc'd us together in an email with the details of the vacant flat. From Melbourne I'd typed the address into Google and hit 'street view'. I'd thought the elms of the park looked pretty. Even with its peeling white paint, in its own way, the house was too. In the image there was broken furniture in the front yard and a man sitting on the stoop. I zoomed in. Though his face was blurred he was waving, like he was saying, 'Come in.' I said I would take the room.

Once I'd arrived and attended a campus orientation I heard that there were rapes and muggings, infamously and semi-regularly, often inflicted on the same victim at the same time, in the park across the road. I only went there if I was running late to workshop, only in daylight, moving fast, cutting straight through.

Our next-door neighbour was a trans woman named Cyndi who smoked menthols in her yard wearing a dull, fraying, peach-coloured satin robe. The downstairs tenants were a young white family who fought constantly, believed Zhen and I were lovers and once threw a small television through their front window.

That afternoon I sat at the top of the steps and felt the summer before me, what it might hold. I took my shirt off and opened Zhen's laptop on my thighs. Zhen had a teaching fellowship for the summer, and when he was out I used his laptop, because I felt anxious, like I should be writing, when I used my own. I scrolled Craigslist. Some listings gave phone numbers, but most gave an option to contact the lister through relayed email addresses. I sent messages to posters with jobs that were largely variable, both in what would be required of me and what I would be paid.

Sitting there, I watched the mother from downstairs, in denim hotpants and a tank top, pushing her twins' double stroller back and forth. There was no sidewalk, so she walked up and down by the edge of the road. She often did this, never going into the park but walking adjacent. The twins looked to be past the age they should be in a stroller and lay mute, one putting his hand completely into the mouth of the other. I didn't interact with them, because once one of the children had waved at me and I had waved back and the mother had spat at the ground and called me a kiddie fucker. This was our relationship.

I looked at my replies. I had responses from listings for Mighty Taco, a caretaker for an aged care village and an attendant who would help take groups of trained corgis to summer weddings. I called the number for the dogs.

'I think there's been a misunderstanding,' a woman said. 'I don't run a business. I just want six corgis at my wedding.'

'Oh.'

'I need to go now, my child is crying.'

My only regular work came from Cyndi, who paid me five dollars a week to stop by her house every morning and take photos of her breasts. She had begun taking hormones and each day her breasts were slightly larger than the day before. She stood in her kitchen and undid her robe, then I would take a photo with a disposable camera and she would say, 'Keep going.' Cyndi posed. She did pirouettes. Then she would say, 'Enough,' and retie the robe.

I liked Cyndi. She was beautiful with dark hair, green eyes. Every morning she had a stale croissant and coffee like she was Audrey Hepburn in *Breakfast at Tiffany's*.

As she ate she liked to hear about the things I had to do. She was interested in the creative writing program, mainly I think because she found the university and its students impractical, partly unreal. I gave her the password to our wifi network and emailed her my stories, though we didn't speak about them.

I told Cyndi how I'd read an interview with a writer who said he paid his rent in the seventies by giving his landlord blow jobs in the stairwell. I myself had been having disappointing sex in America for the past two years but had got little from it. 'I don't think that's so bad,' I said. 'He was living in the Village.'

'Maybe,' she said, 'but have you ever met your landlord?'

Neither of us had. I wasn't sure I had one. Every month I deposited rent into an account. When there was a problem, Zhen and I lived with the problem. Above Cyndi's kitchen there was a room she had barricaded shut with a chest of drawers. Inside was a broken window and sometimes a racoon. She didn't contact anyone about it.

I said, 'I guess that probably wouldn't happen anymore.'

'A blow job doesn't make sense now,' she said. 'I mean, economically.'

When she finished her croissant she put on a white shirt with a mandarin collar and tied her hair back. She was younger than me, but how much younger was hard to say. She was dressing for work, though she wouldn't tell me what she did. When I asked, she'd evade: 'I work with animals.'

Sitting in her kitchen, I knew I wasn't making enough money and she knew it too. I said she didn't have to pay me, but she slipped five one-dollar bills into the elastic of my shorts and said, 'This is America, baby.' Then she walked to the bus stop.

The listing was simple: 'Night Work. Pays in Cash.' I had grown to like simple ads. Even when they lacked an actual description they were at least simple as advertised and the listers weren't fussy. The word 'work' in the listing sounded promising. The things I had been doing prior were difficult to define as work and thus I believed the pay for the job would be higher and possibly more regular. I sent my number.

Cyndi thought night work sounded like the mob or maybe a serial killer, and when I said a serial killer wouldn't advertise on Craigslist she shrugged her shoulders and replied, 'Actually, that's factually incorrect.'

We were sitting in her kitchen. Sitting there, my phone rang. I had a short interview. A man asked me if I was the kind of person who said yes to things. I said, 'Yes.' Then he asked if I could move furniture. I said, 'Yes.' He gave me a time and address. I had the job.

That night Zhen came home from teaching and sat, shirtless and in basketball shorts, writing in the living room. The living room was a kind of communal space neither of us used. I wanted to ask him to write in his room. I didn't like seeing him write, his fingers hitting the keyboard like he was having a great time, like he was having the best time in the world, but I didn't say anything because I was going out.

I left the house in trainers, shorts and a grey American Apparel *Paris Review* t-shirt I felt self-conscious wearing around Zhen. I took a bus to the address, an apartment on South Avenue. When I arrived it was close to ten.

The apartment looked a lot like my room—that is, bare, with cheap wall-to-wall carpeting. The man was maybe a decade older than me, or he liked to tan. His skin creased like leather. He wore a singlet. His name was Vince. He walked me to the back of the lot to his van. I didn't want to get into his van but he asked me to get into the van and I said, 'Yes.'

We drove a while in silence and then he put the radio on. I noticed a dreamcatcher hanging from his rear-view mirror. I asked him if he was Native American. He didn't say anything to that, just turned up the volume.

We pulled into a parking lot close to the lake. The building there was a series of units laid out in a horseshoe, the concrete courtyard between them filled with plastic deck chairs bleached brittle in the sun. He had keys. He told me to wait in the van. He walked into a unit, came back, and told me to follow him. He gave me a flashlight and told me that if anyone asked who we were, the only answer I was to give was to shine my light in their face and say, 'The police.'

We entered unit 2A. Inside the rooms were filled with trash—furniture, broken electronics, boxes. It was like the duplex when Zhen and I moved in. Vince turned towards me. 'This is it. We clear it.'

We moved everything into the van, and when we were done Vince walked around taking photos with his phone. He took photos of ripped-out patches of carpet, holes in the drywall, a red stain marring the kitchen's yellowed laminate floor.

Then we got back into the van and drove until we approached the city's municipal dump, driving alongside it until Vince turned off-road and a line of chain-link fencing flashed in the van's headlights. We got out. Vince walked to the fence and pulled at it. The fencing had been cut. An entire panel of the fence peeled back like a page. We opened the van and carried shit through. We carried it in the dark until we reached the landfill proper, then we dumped it.

The idea was getting refuse into the landfill without having to pay to put it there. If this was illegal it didn't strike me as particularly illegal. I didn't feel like we were breaking any law that mattered. As we worked I thought of myself not as I often did, as a character in a short story, but as a character in a low-budget reality-TV show, something that played in the early hours of the morning.

At the end of the night, he dropped me off at my house and handed me fifty dollars. He said, 'Come back tonight.' It was 4 a.m. The next morning he told me the same thing.

When I didn't have money all I thought about was money, and when I did have money I took Cyndi out to get frappés. Cyndi showed me the bus to the mall. We took it.

The shopping mall was on the edge of the city's lake and seemed to have been designed by someone unfamiliar with the lake, food courts looking out at the water, wide glass windows, elevated viewing platforms. You couldn't swim in the lake because it was filled with industrial run-off and heavy metals. Anyone could tell this by looking at it. The water was the colour of shit, or sometimes unnaturally bright, pearlescent, its surface slicked with oil. But the mall had some things going for it: like every summer, this one was the hottest on record and the mall had AC.

Families who couldn't holiday at the Great Lakes came up to holiday here, and I saw them, flesh overflowing bikinis, guts paunched over nylon shorts, children a blur of pink skin and teeth and noise. They couldn't swim in the lake, but they could at the pool in the mall. They could also drive go-carts. The place confused me on a conceptual level.

Cyndi and I walked into Sephora. When we were in an aisle, alone, no employees watching, Cyndi took a compact case off a shelf, then a kind of blush and a coral-shaded lipstick, and put them in her bag.

As we neared the security guard she turned to me. 'I know it's hard for you,' she said, 'but act cool.'

At Starbucks I remembered a reading Zhen had given organised by the program's faculty. I had not wanted to go but did. In the bar, he read, 'I wrote this in a Starbucks in Shanghai. On the bank of the Huangpu.' It wasn't an aside or introduction, it was two lines of the poem. I was in a Starbucks and I wasn't writing any poems. I wasn't writing anything.

Almost every day I talked to Cyndi about this, and she would say, 'Okay, yes, yes, sure, I get you.' I asked Cyndi again if she had read my stories yet and she sipped her frappé and said, 'No, not yet,' then changed the topic of conversation. Neither of us said much on the bus ride home.

My only measurement of time passing was that once a week Cyndi and I took a bus in the opposite direction to the mall and went to Walgreens, where, under dim fluorescents, Cyndi would drop off a roll of film and collect the prints from the week before.

Whether we went to the mall or Walgreens or Cyndi had work, every morning I took a photo of Cyndi and eventually walked up the stairs to my flat and sat at my desk.

I wanted from the MFA what most people want from most things, that is, total fulfilment of the self. It wasn't lost on me that every day Cyndi became more of herself, realising her potential, while I did not. Thinking this, I would remember that I was the worst kind of writer, the one who took the stories of others and used them as metaphors to illuminate themselves.

Every night once the sun set I took a series of buses to Vince's place and then we drove to houses, condos and flats, driving on the interstate, sometimes alongside the black water of the lake, the shut-down air-conditioner factory or through the streets of the city and then residential suburbs, houses pushed back from the street lights, deep in overgrown yards. We'd clear them, head to the dump, doubling back if we needed to. On a good run we could clear two a night.

We worked as part of an operation, but it took me a while to figure out what the operation was. Vince sent the photos he took to someone and sometimes answered phone calls and gave brief reports. When I asked who he spoke to he said there was a woman in LA with money to make.

As far as I understood, properties foreclosed on years ago were bought from the banks, and then sold and resold through managed funds. People moved or were evicted and left things behind: stained futons, busted-up shopping trolleys, pieces of drywall, a La-Z-Boy recliner with a blood-stain running down its side, *Jane Fonda's Workout* VHS tapes, a faded, cotton-candy-pink jacuzzi, a still-warm hibachi grill, faeces, human faeces, a Donald Trump Halloween mask.

When the properties sat empty, vagrants circled, then squatted. Often services were still connected. We cleared the properties, Vince wrote up false invoices for the municipal dump, and the woman paid him, labour plus fees, then rented the properties at inflated rents to new tenants, ideally people like me, students from the university.

I didn't know if this was all the woman—if she was the owner or just worked for someone else. In a way, everyone works for someone else, and if they don't they work within something else, something bigger. Systems, I thought. It's about the systems. The economy.

I felt ambivalent about it. I didn't feel like I was getting writing material, I was just doing labour. That was fine by me.

As I took the photo of Cyndi one morning, my t-shirt already clung to my back. It was mid-July now. When Cyndi went to work I went back to my room to write, but the humidity was too much. I conserved energy, stayed inside, placed ice cube after ice cube on the back of my neck, made use of Zhen's laptop, his digital subscriptions—*n+1*, *The New Yorker*—stopped reading and scrolled their online stores, considered buying a tote bag. I thought about new story ideas but then thought I would be better able to write them at some unspecified point in the future. I forgot the story ideas. I napped.

When I woke up it was the late afternoon. Outside my window I could see the mother in the front yard, lying on a towel, talking into her phone. She was wearing a bikini. The children sat in the grass next to her, dazed, their skin watermelon pink. I watched her pick up a spray hose, hose one child off and then the other, then put the hose down. I thought I saw movement in the park but I looked closer and it was just heat coming off the road.

I went into the living room. I noticed Zhen's bike was in the living room. Zhen's bike was not meant to be in the living room until he rode it home from teaching.

His door was shut too, which was unusual. The door was only shut when he was sleeping. Even when he was writing he left the door open, like a taunt. He must have come back into the house while I was asleep.

I thought, That's okay, he's asleep. I had taken his laptop from his desk and had intended, like always, to put it back before he got home. I crept into my room, picked it up, considered quietly opening Zhen's door, decided against it—too bold—and placed the laptop on the kitchen counter where he sometimes used it as he cooked.

When I was midway back to my room, his door opened and there was Zhen.

We stood facing each other, then he said, 'Have you been using my laptop?'

I tried to act cool. 'Zhen,' I said, 'why would I use your laptop? I have a laptop.'

We looked at each other. Zhen's eyes narrowed.

I said, 'You're home very early.'

He considered this. Then he said that today the teen-agers didn't want to write stories in the heat. They didn't seem to want to write stories at all, but today there was an excuse, so he had sent them home.

'Wait,' I said. 'Stories? You're teaching fiction?'

'Yes.'

'Not poems?'

'Not poems.'

'But you're not in the fiction track,' I said.

'It doesn't really matter what track you're in,' he said. 'I don't think anyone cares.'

'Some people care,' I said. 'Some people care.' I didn't know what to say next, so I just strode back to my room and closed the door.

Sitting in the passenger seat of Vince's van, I knew, even in the dark, that we were parallel to the park, my park. It's a big park that crosses over many blocks, and I didn't recognise my street until we were in front of the duplex. I asked what we were doing and Vince said, 'What we always do.' He got out of the car but he didn't walk to my house, he walked to Cyndi's. He pulled a key from his pocket and opened the front door.

Vince turned on the lights and I hoped Cyndi wasn't there. Vince walked through the rooms, the front room, the lounge, the kitchen. It was obvious someone was living there. An open box of chow mein sat on the island bench, beside it a glamour magazine and a disposable camera. I heard music coming from down the hall. He pulled out his flashlight and walked up the stairs. With each empty room we entered I felt relieved, but I knew she was home.

He opened the bathroom door, me close behind. First we saw four tea lights flickering on the sink, then a figure in the tub.

Cyndi screamed. Vince swung his flashlight. The beam of light hit her in the face, the light glinting across droplets on her skin. I could see her pupils constrict and felt something like a dead weight plummeting through my chest and stomach. She raised a hand.

'It's the police,' Vince said, his voice muffled. 'Get out.'

She stood up, water sloshing below. She swallowed, tensed her shoulders, squinted. She looked past the light. She saw me. She recognised me.

'You're not the police. Get out of my fucking house.'

'This isn't your house,' Vince said, his voice kidnapper-low. 'You're an illegal occupant. Put something on, then leave.'

'Turn the light off, motherfucker.' She stepped out of the tub. She nodded at me. 'You're working for a fucking slum lord.'

I didn't move. She watched me not move. I watched her bite down on her lip.

Vince didn't turn towards me. He didn't turn towards me because I wasn't a problem, not even a hypothetical one. He spoke again, calm. 'This house isn't yours.'

'Get out.'

'This house isn't yours. You are illegally squatting.'

'And you're trying to illegally evict me. Busting in like SWAT, trying to intimidate me. I'm not an idiot.'

She found a towel and walked towards us. Vince stepped away. I stepped away. She walked past us, continued down the hall and into her bedroom, water puddling on the floorboards. She shut the door behind her. We heard a drawer pulled open.

Vince looked worried, started moving to the stairs. 'We have to leave, now.'

I didn't think she had a gun. I knew she didn't have a gun. I knew she had a hair straightener and no extension cord, but I didn't say these things aloud.

Vince started running. I followed. He yelled out over his shoulder, 'I'll be back tomorrow.'

Cyndi's voice boomed behind us. 'Come, either of you, and I'll taser you. I'll taser you right in the face.'

Outside I crossed the road and vomited onto the lawn of the park.

Vince watched me. When I was done he said we had another address to visit.

I shook my head and climbed the stairs to my flat.

In the morning I went over to Cyndi's. The doors were locked. She wouldn't answer my texts, my calls, so I climbed into the house through the broken second-storey window. Climbing the railing, I was worried someone would call the police. I was worried I'd be shot. If there was a racoon inside, it didn't show itself to me. I jimmied out the chair blocking the door. Cyndi wasn't there.

In the lounge she had written on the wall in coral lipstick. The message was for me, slick and glossy, the letters the size of dinner plates. 'YOUR STORIES ARE SHIT.'

I read the message, read it again, nodded, and walked into the kitchen. Cyndi's hormones were gone. Her photos too. I ate the leftover noodles on the bench. I knew she wouldn't come back.

I called Vince and told him I couldn't work for him anymore. Vince called me many names and I didn't say anything back because I felt they were deserved, even if not from him. Vince owed me a week's pay but told me to go fuck myself.

That night a storm broke, far away, past the lake, with dry lightning. I could see Vince from my room's narrow window, walking in and out of Cyndi's with a man I didn't recognise. I watched in the dark. It was past 1 a.m. I didn't go outside to hassle them. I looked over the park and towards the lake.

I saw a flash of light and waited for thunder.

Within two weeks I had run out of money and could take comfort in the need to survive. It was easier not to write than confront the fact I was doing it poorly. I had a little less than three weeks left of the break. There were emails I sent to Cyndi, texts. I told her she could stay at my rental. She didn't reply. I thought about what Cyndi thought of my stories. Cyndi is not a literary critic, I thought. Even the worst workshop critique would not say that, 'Shit.' It was unjustified. Cyndi had a lot to work out.

When I emailed my professors I got automatic replies or no reply at all. I decided to visit the faculty offices. It was the afternoon. I didn't know what I wanted. Maybe I could plead my case. I power-walked through the park then came onto the campus, approached the limestone belltower of the English department. I couldn't get into the building. Everyone was gone, even the cleaners. I didn't know where Zhen taught his high school students. The only movement I saw was the sudden burst of automated sprinklers across the quad.

I left the grounds and walked to the supermarket. Inside the air-conditioned aisles I saw one of my professors, Claire. This seemed like a good sign. This was where I was meant to be.

Claire was an adjunct with dark skin and even darker hair. Her lips were always chapped and in winter she always wore the same chequered teal-and-red sweater. I noticed her from a distance, down an aisle, and walked towards her. She had got her MFA and released her first novel very young. Once she had got drunk at a reception for a visiting author and I had asked her age and she'd told me, and I left the conversation because we were the same age and I was ashamed. Her cart held two jars of olives and a can of diced tomatoes. We were in the pasta aisle. She spent a long time looking at the prices, her lips pressed together.

'Hey,' I said.

'Oh, hi. You must rent around here too.'

'Yeah.'

She smiled and looked back at the price labels.

'What did you do for the summer?' I asked.

'What I always do: write, hope I have a job come August.' She picked up a box of spaghetti. It was the cheapest brand. She put the spaghetti back down.

I asked, 'Do you know where the faculty are?'

'Probably writing or with their families.'

I nodded. 'I'm looking for things to do.'

She said, 'Write.'

'I was hoping I was going to teach for the summer, but I didn't get classes.'

'If you don't write, no one will let you teach. You can stop writing once you start teaching, right, but you can't get a teaching post without first writing.'

'I guess.' I picked up a bag of rice.

'Anyway, teaching's overrated.'

'Maybe,' I said. 'I think I just need money right now. Do you need anyone to walk your cat?'

'I can't afford a cat.'

'Oh.' I don't know why I said it, but I asked, 'Do you want to get a frappé?'

She looked up at me. 'No, I want to finish shopping and go home.' She pushed her trolley and moved away.

At the register my card was declined. I was buying the bag of rice. I said, 'That's embarrassing,' and sort of smiled at the cashier like we were in on a joke, but the cashier did not smile back and I said, 'I'll just be a minute,' and she took the rice and put it behind the counter and I left the store.

Outside I saw Zhen. He waved. He was across the street wheeling his bike alongside him, holding a brown paper bag gently against his chest. He crossed the street.

I asked what was in the bag.

He opened it and I saw a crinkle of gold foil. It was a bottle of champagne. It was not cheap champagne. I asked what it was for.

Zhen gave a small smile. 'My novel,' he said. 'I finished the first draft.'

I did not know that Zhen was writing a novel. I asked what it was about.

It was about internet venture capitalists in Shanghai, Zhen told me. It was written in the first-person plural, was a little under four hundred pages long and dealt with the modern legacy of Mao.

I said, 'That's great,' and he said, 'It is great,' and I said, 'Great.'

'I mean, it's okay,' he said. 'Maybe the novel isn't very good.'

'No,' I said. 'It's great.'

We walked like this, me repeating 'Great,' all the way home.

That night, after drinking the entire bottle alone, Zhen fell asleep in the living room, his laptop open next to him. Slowly I slid it off the couch and picked it up.

I opened Finder. I did a document search, typing in 'novel'. Nothing came up. I typed in 'Mao'.

When I opened the file, the light of the screen shifted, became dense with type. I sat there, still, reading one page then another. I won't describe them.

In that moment I felt many things. Desolate. Existential. But I had felt all of these things before, and will, I'm sure, feel them again. At one point in my life the MFA had been an escape hatch and I took it, but then I was inside the escape hatch and it was just like being anywhere else.

I closed the document and loaded Craigslist. I found the interface calming, the empty space. I told myself I had to keep going. I went somewhere I had been avoiding. I went to the personals. Most of the ads were for women and seemed to insinuate sex or the possibility of payment for services. I needed money and felt the need to be bold. The morals of the transactions seemed clear to me. Simple.

I went into the bathroom, lifted my shirt and looked at myself in the mirror. Even after almost two months of physical labour I still had the body of a graduate student: nervous, pallid skin, skinny but with fat that had congealed around the back of my hips. I thought, Yes, I am prepared to sell my body and I am prepared to lie over the internet about the state that body is in.

I went back to the laptop and started typing. I made my own listing. Posted it. I wrote that I was a college student trying to make it in the world. I said I played sports I had never played, sports like gridiron, lacrosse and soccer, and when a forty-six-year-old messaged me an hour later asking if I wanted to 'play' I said yes, but that I only played with gifts. He wrote back, 'Okay I'm coming.' I sent the address. It was after midnight.

While I waited, lying on my bed, I thought, Mary Gaitskill, Mary Gaitskill, and dressed in what I imagined a college student would wear: Zhen's basketball shorts, my American Apparel *Paris Review* tee.

When the man arrived he told me he only had a credit card. I nodded and quickly ushered him into my room.

The man was black, overweight, had a thin moustache and smelt not unpleasantly of Old Spice. I didn't know if I should play a part, be naïve, but settled on a businesslike tone. I thought fast. I said the man could come with me to buy groceries, that the store was just down the road. He was quiet for a moment and then said, 'Okay.' I repeated, 'Yes.' I began pulling down his sweatpants. Neither of us seemed very aroused.

Afterwards the streets were empty, and the man stared at his feet as we walked, or occasionally looked up, apprehensively, at the shadows of the park. It was warm out. I directed us to the supermarket that was further away but sold things in economy sizes. It was shut. We walked to the other supermarket, which was twenty-four hours. The man seemed nice but out of breath. I noticed wet patches slowly grow beneath his arms. I could feel dried cum on my stomach.

Inside I filled my grocery cart with full-cream milk, bread, eggs, orange juice. The man asked if I could hurry. I should have been sensible, grabbed a five-kilo bag of lentils. Instead I got what I felt I deserved. Walking to the registers, I picked up an on-sale twelve-bottle pack of San Pellegrino sparkling water.

The items came to twenty-eight dollars. The man blushed as he took out his card. We left separately. No one was on the street. No one approached me. No one jumped out to stab me from the park.

At home Zhen was snoring on the couch. I put the shopping away and threw Zhen's shorts into his laundry pile.

I sent a text to Cyndi. She didn't reply. I showered, feeling pleased with myself, my ingenuity.

I lay in the dark of my room and drank sparkling water from the bottle.

Four days later I'd run out of food. Again, Zhen had left his laptop in the living room. I took it to my room and checked my listing's messages. There was one from a man in his twenties.

The guy who came over looked younger, maybe nineteen. He was white, had bloodshot eyes and wore worn-out Air Jordans. It was 2 a.m. He sat on my bed, fidgeted, watched as I undressed and said, 'What are you, like, over thirty?'

'I'm twenty-nine,' I said.

'That's pretty old.'

'It really isn't,' I said.

'I'll still fuck you but I'm not happy about it.'

I pretended we were being coquettish. I mentioned money, cash. He said we could talk about that later and asked for something to drink.

I held my t-shirt in front of my crotch, walked into the kitchen and filled a glass with sparkling water. I recognise now that this was a poor decision.

I heard movement and turned. He was crossing the living room. He was running. His hands gripped something flat and metallic. It was Zhen's laptop. I yelled. I charged. He pivoted and with one fist, jabbed me in the throat. My legs gave way. The glass fell, shattered. He was gone.

I pulled myself up. The front door was open. I ran onto the landing. I could see him across the road, and then he was swallowed by the elms of the park. I stood there, naked, my penis inexplicably erect.

Zhen came out of his room. He kept his eyes level with mine. He asked, 'Where is my laptop?' I didn't say anything. Calmly, he told me that I should move. 'Also,' he said, 'your feet are bleeding.'

The next day we had a long and difficult discussion. Zhen wanted me to leave and was considering reporting my conduct to the university, but I could tell he was conflicted. I told him I was conflicted too. I said that I was horrified and sorry I had caused him to lose so much work, and he interrupted and said that he wasn't an idiot, that his work was all on the cloud. I told him that I would buy him a new laptop, and that in the interim, while I gathered the funds, he could have mine. His face was hard to read. Then I told him I would give him time to work on his novel: I would mark his students' papers.

Zhen said, 'Okay.'

And so that night Zhen gave me a pile of printed stories, and another the next night, and the next. The stories were bad. The kind of stories that no matter what was done to them they would never be good. I was intimately familiar with this type of story. I wrote notes like, 'This image!' and 'Careful with your tenses.' Next to a line that was just a line like any other I drew a smiley face. I wrote, 'This is a great story, you should consider an MFA.'

Zhen didn't read the notes. He thanked me and let me subsist off packets of noodles from his shelf in the kitchen. At night I heard the downstairs tenants screaming. I lay in bed waiting for something terrible and final to reach me, but the only thing I could think of was the end of the program and the expanse that came after.

And then, lying there, late one night, I looked at my phone. My stipend had been deposited into my account and I felt that life was beautiful. I felt a rush.

Lydia texted me. She was back from Maine. 'Where are you? There's a party.'

Zhen and I went to the party. Bodies moved to music. Someone had got a keg. Outside, a woman rested on her haunches by the side of the road. She was peeing into the gutter. She looked up. It was Lydia.

The next day Lydia wanted to do something that would commemorate our summers. She said we should have a spa day, her treat. My hands were calloused, my feet blistered. I wanted a spa day. I felt good about it. Zhen came too.

We took a bus to the mall, Lydia repeating, 'Are you sure this goes to the mall?'

I thought it was stupid that Lydia had lived here two years but didn't know how to get to the mall. Then I remembered that I hadn't, either. I didn't know if anyone else in the program would. The city wasn't our city. It was a nondescript setting.

I asked if she'd finished any stories and she said, 'Let's not talk about stories.' I smiled. Whatever slump I'd gone through over the summer was going to turn around. I could turn around.

At the mall we went to the nail salon. A woman led us to three large armchairs then gave us towels and cucumber water. The staff wore mandarin collars.

Lydia asked, 'Can you guys do a mimosa?'

The woman said, 'No.'

Lydia turned to me. 'We'll make them later.'

The woman asked what we wanted.

I said I wanted a pedicure.

Zhen said, 'We'll have the most expensive one.' It was forty dollars.

The woman took off Zhen's slides, held his foot in one hand then gently placed it in a tub of hot water.

I looked down and there was Cyndi. She nodded at me as she set down my tub. There were a lot of things I didn't say that should have been said. I put my feet in the water and asked if she had really felt that way about my stories.

She bit her lip and said, 'Paul, I didn't read your stories.'

I said, 'Oh.'

'It's not a big deal,' she said. Then, turning my foot to the side, she said, 'No one will.'

This felt right to me. I mean, it was true.

Life Coach

I took a connection from Beijing to Zhengzhou, and there, waiting at the arrivals gate, was the life coach. He was not my life coach. I did not need a life coach, but I admired him, his path. We had met in Melbourne at a large outdoor dance party. He was travelling. He stopped me as we danced, his eyes dilated, took my phone from my hand, typed in his Instagram handle and pressed follow. Since then we'd messaged each other every now and then, which made me feel sophisticated, international.

From his online presence I knew he was certified by the GCA, the Global Coach Association, had a low body mass index and offered a range of coaching packages. On his website were testimonials and photos of himself in professional yet tight-fitting shirts. He was a very spiritual person and communicated this on his 'About' page by saying, 'I am a very spiritual person.'

When he saw me at the arrivals gate I knew he was disappointed. He stared at my lazy eye and spoke sullenly as if I had deceived him. This felt unfair to me as we'd already met. I told him where my hotel was and he said, 'That's quite far away.'

In the car, driving, he relaxed and spoke about himself, largely things he'd already told me: that he was in Asia working on himself but that working on himself had become lucrative, as he had become the live-in coach for a Texan businesswoman and a Foxconn executive, and that he had a set of clients back home in America whom he consulted via lengthy video calls.

I was interested because this was the kind of work I felt destined to do and in this way we were peers. I nodded, made mental notes and looked out at the mountains, the freeway seven lanes across, the bikes, and, once we were in the city, what I thought was a large stadium but was actually a palatial railway station. The life coach would not look at me. At stop lights he looked in the dashboard mirror and fixed his hair. Though the sky was already dark, I put my sunglasses on, acted cool.

In the hotel's parking lot I asked if he wanted to come upstairs. This was sexual. The next day I would be in a monastery and so I believed I should indulge. I tried to make this clear. He said he couldn't, he was getting dinner with friends. I asked if I could join. He said, 'It's better if you rest.'

My room was on the fifth floor and looked out over the hotel's parking lot. I could stand by the window and see the life coach in his parked car.

An hour went by. I took off the money belt I had promised my mother I would wear, shoved it into my coat pocket, showered, flicked through television channels in a language I didn't understand, drank an orange soda from the minibar, did some push-ups, flexed naked in front of the bathroom mirror and went back to the window. He was still there. I opened Grindr. I could see his profile, fifty metres away.

His profile was a photo of him, shirtless, kneeling, mouth open, looking up at the camera.

I messaged, 'I can see you.' I think I saw him move in his car but at a distance it was hard to tell. Then I messaged again. 'Do you want to get dinner?'

He replied, 'I'm good.'

I was in China for the same reason the life coach was: to grow.

At home I never drank alcohol, smoked or took substances. I drank herbal teas, exercised compulsively, ate only organic and devoted most of my time to helping people. I did this by posting on self-help forums.

The site I used had different boards for separate but often interrelated things: Health, Relationships, Career. Because I had replied to such a large number of posts I was what was known on the site as a 'super guru'. This was shown as a kind of green glow, an aura, that encircled my profile photo, which was a nondescript picture of a clear sky.

I would log onto the site, light a stick of incense, watch the smoke coil then reply to people's problems, meditating on them, sometimes consulting TikTok videos, clips of daytime talk shows, only coming out of my room when my mother asked me to set the table or walk the family toy poodle, which I would do quietly, contemplatively, and then return to my laptop.

I was eighteen and unemployed, had barely graduated high school and scored poorly on standardised and non-standardised tests, but when I was on the site no one ever asked for credentials.

I replied to a range of things. A woman said she was full of worms but that her doctor would do nothing about it. The doctor thought she was crazy. Using a douche, she squirted tea-tree oil up her anus. It burned. I wrote, 'Keep douching. Take charcoal tablets three times a day.'

A man posted that at thirty-two he was finally working in advertising, the field of his dreams, but that his workplace demeaned him. It was a very long post. One day his manager couldn't find him in the office and so had called the man's mobile. The man was at home replying to emails and watching a drama series set in a fictional advertising agency. His manager told him that he could not work from home, that he was only an assistant at the agency, that his contract stipulated that he would come into the office three days a week, and that, yes, while other employees sometimes did work from home they were full-time employees and their contracts had work-flex clauses that his did not. He was told that he could come in another day that week to make up the shift or he could have the day as personal leave.

I typed, 'If these people don't respect you now they will never respect you. Quit. This is the year of you. You're worth it.'

Those were the things I answered. Things like that.

My parents, two modest financial planners, often wanted to discuss my plans going forward, and I would tell them I was doing what the universe wanted me to be doing but that people were ageist, distrusting, and so I had to wait until I was a little older before I would self-start my own coaching business, before I could take on seed money and paying clients. But I was also thinking about it a lot in the meantime, thinking it all out.

It was on an evening like this that I became frustrated. I told my parents that I knew a lot of things—things I had learned listening to podcasts—like how to make a million dollars, how to take risks for what you believed in, how to confront one's soul. And my father said, 'Okay, well, maybe you should try the first thing. It would be great if you made a million dollars.'

And I nodded aggressively and said, 'Sometimes I'm so excited about my life, all the things I'm going to do, my heart beats fast and I choke up.'

My mother said, 'That's very nice.'

I said, 'I'm choking up,' and went back to my room.

My mother brought me a glass of water. I drank the water and opened my laptop. I felt I had to do something. Because of the sites I visited, online advertisements often suggested certain kinds of things: new dietary supplements, reiki healers, meditation retreats in Bhutan, Thailand, Hawaii. And though I knew this was algorithms, data streams merging with my browsing history, I understood it to also, at times, be connected to a deeper meaning, my desires made manifest. That night an ad for a Buddhist monastery showed itself in the left bar of my browser window. It was deep in China, in Henan, on the slope of a tall mountain. The life coach was also in China, I knew, vaguely near said mountain, and I took this as a sign.

Though I didn't work, I had some money. For my birthday my parents had given me a modest sum, three thousand dollars, they wanted me to bank as a term deposit. I didn't use it as a term deposit. I saw it could be better spent as an investment. All I had to do was recite my debit card details and follow a series of links as the links were presented to me.

That I didn't speak Mandarin wasn't a problem or particularly remarkable. I had a piece of hotel stationery on which the receptionist had written the name of the town of my connection and then the name of the monastery, all in Chinese. I pointed to one and then the other and found myself on one bus and then a second, smaller bus that snaked its way up the mountain, skirting the sudden drop of a cliff face, everything on the mountain covered in pure white snow.

I arrived at the monastery and stood outside its gates. Snow dusted the tiled roof and the tiers of the pagoda that rose behind it. I waited with my luggage.

A monk came out. He began to speak to me and I began to speak to him but we couldn't understand each other. The monk left.

The monk returned with a second monk. We spoke in English.

The second monk told me there had been a miscommunication over dates. The monk said the monastery was full but that there would soon be space for me. There was a Western-style youth hostel in the town and I could stay there and wait. There was also a boarding house at the base of the mountain but the hostel was far more comfortable, the monk said. The hostel had internet. I wanted to impress them so I told them I didn't want for comfort. The boarding house would be sufficient.

The first monk drove me down the mountain in a pick-up truck, only our headlights lighting the way.

The boarding house sat next to the road in what looked like an empty field, but at night it was hard to say. I got out of the truck and the monk pointed to the door.

A short woman met me and led me inside. We passed an open room in which an old man holding a lit cigarette watched television, and a dining room with a large table. Everything was very cluttered. She took me up a narrow staircase and at the top was a small window and then a single room.

Inside, beneath a lone fluorescent tube, were two beds, really just two clapboard frames, and between them a small cot. In one bed was a balding German man in a grey robe. He said he wasn't at dinner because he had digestive problems. I went towards the other bed and the German told me it was taken, so I leant my luggage against the wall, looked at the cot on the floor, bunched up my puffy coat and lay down on it.

It was very late. Lying on the cot, I could hear wild dogs howling outside.

When the German was asleep or just staring at the ceiling, I sat up on my cot and did my eye exercises, then watched a show I'd saved onto my phone. At home I watched a series of similar dramas in which things happened to people requiring doctors—who sometimes slept with each other—to operate on them, or emergency services personnel—who sometimes slept with each other—to save them. But I'd only saved one episode, so I watched it once and then watched it again. Like a first responder, I felt very selfless. I felt it was my duty to help people, and that where I was, what I was doing, would be used to help them in the future.

When the episode ended, my other roommate entered the room. He said his name was Jacob. He looked like he was my age or slightly older. I said, 'Hi.' He took his shirt off. He was jacked. He started doing push-ups. The room was a small room. He was very close to me.

He looked at me. He said, 'Are those AirPods?'

I said, 'Yes.'

Then he said, 'That's a nice phone,' and I don't know why, but instead of saying yes what I did was give a little bow.

The boarding house was at the foot of the mountain, and from the second-floor landing, beside the hallway that led to my room, you could see the hills, the beginning of the mountain and the steel beams of a construction project. There was some snow but it was mainly sleet that came down and turned the fields to mud. I could see the road that joined the mountain to the town, and draped above it, a single powerline.

Jacob and the German went into the town every day, but I didn't know what they did there. On my first day I followed the road to town but I didn't have the right kind of shoes. I had tennis shoes. As soon as I walked outside they were wet. The walk took an hour and when I entered the town a group of schoolchildren began to follow me. They yelled out, 'Hello! Hello!' and giggled, ran away then circled back. It felt like they were making fun of me. I turned around and walked back to the house.

There was a woman who was also staying there. I met her in the courtyard, what was just a square of cracked concrete. She was Canadian, in her early forties, and had a room on the first floor all to herself. She sat under a blanket, her leg elevated on a plastic stool. She had sprained her ankle climbing the steps of the mountain to visit a shrine. Now she was waiting for the ankle to heal before moving on to Yunnan. She sat there reading, drinking tea—healing tinctures the boarding house owner had bought from the herbalist in town. When I looked at her, all I saw were the four prominent blonde hairs growing from her chin.

I nodded to her then went and lay on my cot till dinner. I wore my coat and watched my television episode then came down to dinner recharged.

We ate in the small room on the first floor. We ate the same thing at night that we ate in the morning: small bowls of noodles, some steamed vegetables and tofu steeped in oil. Jacob didn't come down for dinner. Either he was out or he ate packets of potato chips in our room.

The Canadian became chatty at night. She explained that her healer had told her that her dead dog had been her lover in a previous life. In their previous life together they had lived at the foot of a mountain, somewhere in China, but the woman had been married to another man. Their lives had ended violently and then her lover had found her again but she didn't know it was him, and as a dog he couldn't figure out a way to tell her. She was travelling to different mountains and thought she would recognise hers when she saw it. This made sense to her.

The German had come here because he couldn't get work in Munich and his meditation leader had instructed him to come here. He didn't know what he was doing here exactly, but he did find the mountain very spiritual. The Canadian agreed there was a spiritual feeling.

The German said that on coming here he had visited the Shaolin Temple where he had watched a show in which a woman in red high heels and smudged lipstick yelled at the crowd to buy Shaolin DVDs while teenagers in robes did somersaults and broke cinderblocks in two. The actual monks did not come out. He sensed them, though, hiding behind the walls. He respected that. The German bought two DVDs but so far had not been able to watch them—his laptop lacked a disk drive.

I sat quietly during dinner. I knew I would not take advice from these people because they seemed like people I would help online, desperate people who didn't think things through. It was clear to me that if the German wished to live in Munich he should have studied a course that would have led to employment in Munich. I would recommend moisturising his scalp. That would boost his confidence. The woman, electrolysis. They would both be happier. But I couldn't help them. I mean, I wouldn't. This was a conscious choice I grappled with. While I was there, I was there for me.

Though I found most people there slightly sad; the exception was Jacob. He was twenty and from West Virginia and intended once he went back home to open a personal training business, maybe even a chain.

On my third night, in our room, he told me he was between monastery stays. He had been travelling now for two years. He had been somewhere recently, a kung fu school, and there had been a physical altercation and he had been asked to leave. He said the people there didn't know what they were doing, that it was all for tourists, that they were fools.

He told me he was going to find the real thing, and I said, in a way, that's what I was doing too.

I asked if he knew Buddhism.

'Yes,' he said. He got up from his bed. He spoke very seriously. He said that at a monastery a novice, someone who wanted to follow the Buddha, would shave their head. Then he told me he had an electric razor. He waited for me to ask him to shave my head. I asked him.

We did it in the room, my head bent over a towel.

Because he had already been a novice, he said, he didn't need to shave his head again.

I said, 'Okay,' and watched my hair fall to the ground.

When the lights were off I lay on my cot and ran my hand across my scalp. I repeated affirmations. I asked myself if I had the willpower necessary to realise my aspirations as my reality. I whispered, 'Yes.'

Days passed. The sun went up and down. Whenever the old man saw me he ran his hand across his own head and laughed. Then he would do a thumbs-up. I didn't hear anything from the monastery. I also didn't know how the monastery would contact me—if they would send someone down the mountain or expected me to know intuitively.

One morning before Jacob left for the day I went up to him and said I was ready for more. That I wanted teachings.

He said, 'The world is suffering.'

I said, 'Okay, okay. Easy to remember.' Then Jacob did this thing. It involved one arm, a leg, and I was on the floor. I hit it hard.

'That wasn't very Buddhist of me,' he said.

I stayed on the ground. Something trembled in my throat.

He told me, 'You have an annoying energy. You should work on that.' He helped me up.

Another day I stood in the courtyard, bored, and watched the Canadian.

She was reading a series of books by an American Buddhist nun. I recognised the books because my mother read them. My mother would read the books in bed, think about the disappointments of her life, grip our toy poodle and weep.

I wanted to have the kind of knowledge the book jackets said the nun had—'Knowledge to transform one's self and the world'—but I wanted to learn that knowledge firsthand. I wanted to be able to look at someone and see the deepest recess of their soul. Then I thought perhaps I should read the books in the meantime.

I walked up to her and asked if I could borrow one. The woman said, 'No. I want to read this one.' I asked about another. 'That one too. I think I want to read them all.'

I told her I wanted to have a spiritual experience and she nodded, looked into my eyes and said, 'There are YouTube videos for this.'

Then she told me she hadn't really sprained her ankle. With the toes of her elevated foot she traced a small circle in the air and said, 'I just wanted to rest.' I didn't know who the lie was for, if the lie was for the woman that ran the boarding house or if the lie was for herself. Then she asked why I wanted to have a spiritual experience. I didn't have an answer for that so she asked what I did back home.

I told her I was a life coach. She said, 'A life coach?' And I said, 'Yes,' and she said, 'People come to you and you tell them what to do?' and I said, 'Yes,' and she said, 'You,' and I said, 'Yes, that's right, me.' And then we were quiet for a little while. I thought she might ask me a question about her life, maybe about the dog. She didn't. She let out what I think was a giggle. I went back to my room and frowned.

That afternoon I was impatient.

I took the bus to the monastery and stood before the gate. As soon as someone came out I would ask them if there was space for me. I waited. I could hear the monks in prayer. I had read that the monks could pray for days and nights at a time. It began to snow. I waited a little more. No one came out.

I began to walk, slowly, down the mountain. There was no path, or I couldn't find the path, so I had to walk on the road and press myself up against the rock when a truck or a car passed. It was very cold. My scalp was cold and my feet were wet.

For a while my vision turned white like I was inside a bank of cloud. I stepped off the road and sat down in the snow. I know you're not meant to sit in the snow. I lay down. I looked up. I could see the bare arms of the trees, then white. I shivered. I curled around myself and tried to put my head beneath my arms. It didn't do anything. I thought, I am going to die here.

Then I got up and walked the rest of the way down.

Jacob was talking about leaving the mountain and travelling on.

'I think I am going to go to another monastery too,' I said. I was swaddled in blankets on my cot. I was still shivering. Beneath the blankets I still wore my coat. 'I think that's the right thing to do.'

Jacob was sitting on his bed. 'You're probably not ready for a monastery,' he said. 'The monks know it. They looked at you and could tell.'

I didn't want to have this conversation facing him, so I rolled over. I looked at the other bed.

I said, 'If you visualise me in a monastery you will see me in a monastery.'

'In a monastery you have to leave the material world.'

I said I could do that.

'You have to renounce your possessions.'

I said, 'Okay.'

'You have to say it out loud. You have to say, "I renounce my possessions."'

I repeated it. I said, 'I renounce my possessions.'

'You have to mean it.'

I said, 'I mean it.'

Then Jacob said, 'I'm happy for you. I really am.'

I felt better after eating noodles. I had a second serve, a third. The Canadian and the German were talking about God, that if God was everything then was the table God, and if the table was God would that change how they interacted with it. They couldn't decide. Then I went upstairs. Jacob's things were gone and my luggage was gone. My phone, my passport, my clothes. The only things left were what I was wearing and the few twenty yuan notes tucked into the money belt in my jacket pocket.

I thought, This is a test. Then I waited. Then I realised it was not a test.

————

I lay on my cot as the German snored. I had lain like this for most of the night but I couldn't sleep. I knew I had to leave.

I got up and walked out of the boarding house and onto the road. I followed it, alongside it, walking beneath the powerline and next to it a deep ditch. The road was very dark. I thought I might look into the ditch and see a wild dog but all I saw were shadows. I thought, I am lost, I am lost, then I lost my footing. I fell into the ditch. I climbed out and walked until I reached town.

In town, people were waking and going about their lives. I walked through a small market, passed buildings painted in pink, a soft green, gas tanks piled next to a closed metal door. The sun rose but you couldn't see it. The sky lightened to the same colour as the concrete road.

I passed an internet cafe. There were two bright flags in front of it. I doubled back and walked inside. There were rows of computers and, in front of them, big padded armchairs. I wanted to sit in one. From the entrance I could see a man sleeping, his coat draped over his head like a shroud.

A man was at the front desk. He stopped me. He held up a pink ID card. I shook my head. I put some yuan on the desk. He said something then typed into his phone and held it up. It read, 'Regulation.'

I put some more yuan on the desk. He shook his head. I put all I had on the desk. He didn't budge. I picked up the notes and left.

I wandered. Then I found something: a sign I could recognise.

It was the International Youth Hostel. Inside was a small lobby. There was a girl sitting behind the reception desk, watching something on her phone. To the side of the lobby was a computer. It was just sitting there, its screen on, completely free. I walked up to it and sat down. I pretended I was staying there. I was an international youth staying at the International Youth Hostel. The girl at reception didn't even look at me.

I opened a browser window. I opened the site of the consulate. I shut the site of the consulate. I thought to email my parents but didn't. I typed in the address for my forums. The site wasn't blocked. This seemed like a sign. I logged in. I responded to a post. I said, 'Your husband sounds like a toxic person. Leave him. Contact your phone provider and report his phone number.' Then I responded to another. 'Aspiration leads to actualisation. Good things are coming!' I started moving through posts faster. I got into a rhythm. Rapid fire.

I typed, 'It's okay to spend money if you're helping the economy.' 'Eat less red meat.' My hands were shaking. 'Empower yourself.' 'Consider CrossFit.'

Normally, responding gave me a calm. It settled me, made me feel good. But I didn't feel good. I felt afraid.

I typed to someone, 'Imagine the events of your life as markers on a long road. Think where the road will take you in five years. If you don't like it, correct course accordingly.'

I shuddered. I stopped typing. I was sweating. The cursor blinked.

Then, from the computer, I messaged the life coach in Zhengzhou. He replied almost instantly.

I said the monastery was not going as expected.

He wrote, 'Are you asking for advice?'

I said, 'Yes.'

'Five hundred.'

'What?'

'Pay me. Five hundred dollars. USD.' And then, 'I accept PayPal. Bank transfer.'

I sat in front of the computer. He messaged again. He had things to do. If I didn't want a life coach, if I didn't want to grow, that was fine by him. He said his schedule was very busy. Then he told me he could move things around. Then, after ten minutes, he messaged that he could call now. 'But,' he wrote, 'you need to PayPal me.'

I hesitated. Then I messaged, 'Okay,' and paid what was left of my term deposit.

His face appeared on the screen.

I whispered into the computer. I asked how he became a life coach.

He said, 'No, I want to hear about you,' and when I started he said, 'Actually, I've met you. I know you. I know. Let's go to the deep end. Tell me what is the one thing you want. What you really want.'

I thought about this. 'What I really want,' I said, 'is to help people, but I need them to let me help them. I need to grow.'

'But you're doing it,' he said. 'You reached out. You have a life coach now. That's profound. You don't know it yet, but it is.'

I said, 'Yes.'

He nodded. Then he said, 'What you're doing, you have to ask yourself, is it coming from a place of ego or a place of love?'

I began to speak.

'No, don't answer that,' he said. 'Just think about it. Stay with the thought. I don't want the defence. We're dribbling around the defence. We're past it.'

Then he spoke about how he had overcome certain things, vague forces that had worked against him in his life. There was a complicated story involving his teeth, and about how certain people had said nasty things online, awful things about his teeth, and how he had then got orthodontics.

He said there was a point in his life when he was dirty, cold and alone, rolling around in mud. He said, 'I was literally rolling around in mud and I had to be rolling around in that mud, because it was only when I was in that mud that I knew my life had to change.' He linked this to his once-debilitating fear of public speaking.

I said, 'Okay.'

He said, 'Listen, there wasn't any mud. The mud is a metaphor.' Then he told me to imagine my life as a book. Did I like how the book was going? If I didn't, I was the author, so I had the power to write the next chapter, I could change the plot.

I nodded. I said, 'Correct course, life's a road.'

'Not a road. A book. It's a book,' he said. 'Let's be silent for a little. I want you to think about all of this. Let it sink in.' He looked at his phone. He typed into it.

The life coach said, 'Okay, that's our time.' He then told me that if I wrote him a testimonial—and it would have to be a good testimonial—he would give me a fifteen-minute session for free.

'Write that book,' he said and ended the call.

There were things I had wanted to ask that I hadn't asked. Specific things, like: no one likes me or takes my advice, and I do not have a passport, what should I do?

I figured I knew what to do in the short term and that was write the testimonial.

So I did. I wrote not just what was expected but the things I wanted people to say about me, their gratitude, the things I wanted to believe. I finished with the line, 'He truly changed my life.'

I waited for him to reply and say, 'Yes, let's have our fifteen minutes,' for his face to appear on the screen.

I spent a lot of time in that lobby, and in that time I thought terrible things. I thought, This man is an idiot. I thought, I am an idiot. I thought, I am a fraud and you are a fraud. But then the thoughts passed. I let them go.

I waited for most of the afternoon.

I Feel It

In Majorca, jet-lagged at the airport, Nathan bought a one-litre bottle of Tanqueray, and then, after an hour's drive, their van stopping in a small, possibly medieval town, a second bottle of gin, soda water and limes. They drove further, another half hour, the sea beside them, before reaching the house. The house was isolated, far from town, on the edge of a cliff that plunged into water so clear that from the terrace Nathan could see fish swimming at the water's base.

There was a woman waiting for them. She took them through the house, each room all sparse, white walls, wooden beams across the ceiling. She had all seven of them cram into the bathroom, where she demonstrated flushing the toilet. It was how one usually used a toilet. She said, 'This is very important. One flush.' The woman lingered, untrusting, then left them keys.

They had rented the house for a week, after which they would fly on to Tel Aviv, arriving on the second day of Pride.

Nathan tried to nap in his room. The others slept. Nathan wished he had an Ambien. He imagined the discreet white disk of one, then, failing to sleep, took out his MacBook and began to stream an Éric Rohmer film he had misremembered as being set in the Mediterranean but, watching, realised was set on the beaches of France's other side. Somewhere between the protagonist being filled with longing and the protagonist being filled with more longing, Nathan opened Grindr.

He saw someone else from the house, blocked them, turned over on the bed, and browsed, each square on the screen a different body, each one tens of kilometres away.

The seven of them had flown in from Melbourne, where, on Friday nights, after eating and showering and douching with his body crouched over the shower tiles, Nathan would dress and then go to one of the others' apartments, which would be more or less the same as Nathan's apartment but with a substantially wider balcony. There, Nathan and his friends would laugh, drink, then open small ziplock bags and take—swallow, snort or shelve—what was inside, let whatever substance it was hit, feel high or low, something strobe-like in between, then, all together, head to a club.

At the club he would speak repetitively. 'Yes, yes. I feel it.' He would wait in line for a toilet stall, then, once inside, open the ziplock bag and take a little more. He'd feel a thrill, the world would become iridescent, strange. By 3 a.m., his pupils depthless and dilated, Nathan would move through the bodies on the dance floor, alone. Things would happen. They could involve multiple people or singular. Eventually, he would find himself in a rideshare returning to his apartment as the sky began to swell with dawn.

On Mondays and Tuesdays, coming down, Nathan would navigate his office, hesitant and tactile, his hand brushing against the cool of a whiteboard, a fern. Information in meetings, direct questions, registered at a slight delay, followed by a kind of mental reverb during which Nathan knew he had to respond but couldn't immediately intuit how, sometimes forgetting he could not use emojis face-to-face but had to make the actual gestures, a thumbs-up, a smile, IRL. Back at his desk he would run a series of sentiment reports, stare blankly at the aggregates, then tweet under the company handle, sometimes feeling reckless, anxious, or both.

After work he would walk to a large, multi-storey Virgin Active and use the weight machines, swim in the pool, shower. At home he'd sleep, sometimes stream a film. Wednesday came. Thursday. Money was deposited into his account. Money was debited.

In the morning, they all climbed down the cliff beside the house and sunned themselves like Europeans, the seven of them naked on the rocks, Nathan looking a lot like Jarred who looked a lot like David who looked a lot like Mitch. Nathan swam, then, with his eyes closed, let his body float in the water, languid. The afternoon approached.

Together, they made the two-hour hike into town, where there was a small pebble beach. It was a lot like the beach at the house, but with a large boulder in the middle of the bay. There were a few old Spanish men sitting on cracked plastic chairs, what looked like a British family stepping awkwardly across the pebbles, a young woman in an orange string bikini, the straps untied, indistinct figures further on. Nathan waded to the boulder, then lifted himself onto it. Nathan scanned the other people on the beach, Terminator-style, and assessed whether anyone on the beach or foreshore might fuck him, whether there were prospects for something more, a fling, an amorous encounter. Nathan thought, No, then climbed down.

At the grocery store, they bought more alcohol and paid for double bags. They trekked home, opening low-carb beers as they walked, the sun suspended above the water, inching lower and lower, becoming something breathtaking. The sea and sky turned molten, until the sun crossed the horizon and the light began to drain.

They continued drinking on their terrace, played music, looked up at the stars. Bottles of vodka were emptied, one was accidentally smashed on the ground. Mitch tried to make whiskey sours but somehow jammed the cocktail shaker. Nathan, Mitch and David each wrestled the cocktail shaker, and David fell into a small shrub. Lying there, still in the shrub, David smiled.

Nathan felt a certain energy, an excitement, to be with friends, his emotions joyous and oversized, and then slowly that excitement dissipated. From the house, there was nowhere to go.

The next day, a van drove them to a different town, where they went on a yacht and took photos of one another on the yacht. The yacht was stationary, docked in the marina. This wasn't apparent in the photographs. They drank champagne and walked barefoot on the deck. Mitch Facetimed his boyfriend. The boyfriend was a makeup artist nobody liked because he was young, loud, put his feet up on people's furniture, and spoke mostly about himself, repeated the words 'my life's direction'. Mitch showed his boyfriend the yacht. Nathan avoided being in the frame.

After three days, they were all bored of Majorca. At least, Nathan was bored of Majorca. The others were happy lounging in the heat.

Back at the house, they connected a MacBook to the flat-screen TV and watched episodes of a reality show following the activities of rich women, but only the episodes in which they were on group vacations, vacations that seemed somehow more vivid than Nathan's, or at least better lit. At a mansion in Cartagena, one of the women walked through the courtyard and said, 'This floor is filthy,' and later defecated on it, blaming bad seafood. In Mexico, a different woman was drunk and drove a steak knife into the dining room table. It stuck straight up in the wood. She smiled. Her hand, but not the hand that held the knife, began to bleed. This confused the group and, seemingly, the show's producers.

Nathan got up from the couch and helped David wash glasses.

Someone said it would be funny if the women took psilocybin. Then everyone thought it would be funny if they all took psilocybin and lay on the terrace. Then they realised they couldn't get psilocybin. David said, 'This was poorly planned.'

Then someone said, 'Let's just watch it as if they're on psilocybin.'

In Saint Bart's one of the women looked at a man dressed like a pirate and said, 'That man looks exactly like Johnny Depp.'

Nathan said, 'Definitely on psilocybin.'

Everyone laughed.

They watched the episode filmed after the same woman had been arrested in Palm Beach. She had gone into her hotel room but it was not her hotel room. It was someone else's hotel room. Police arrived. She was escorted to a squad car. The show played the squad-car footage.

The woman sat on the back seat in handcuffs. Then she did something with her hands and she was out of the hand-cuffs. She exited the squad car. An officer told her not to slip out of the handcuffs and cuffed her again. The woman said, 'My love, my love.' She was brought back into the squad car. She said, 'I am going to get you. Big time.' Then she said, 'I am going to kill you. I am going to kill you.' The officer shut the door. Her head lolled forward, then back. She was charged with disorderly conduct, battery and resisting arrest.

Nathan thought, Maybe not psilocybin, but didn't say this aloud.

The group discussed taking the ferry to Barcelona—that one of them could go get drugs in Barcelona and catch the ferry back. Then they found out the ferry trip took seven hours, one way. No one wanted to get the ferry. Jarred, his head resting on Mitch's thigh, said he might, paused, then said, 'Actually, no. I don't think I will.'

Nathan suggested they go to Ibiza. Nathan mispronounced Ibiza.

Mitch replied, 'I mean, it's an option,' and then the subject changed.

———

The next day, they did what they did every day. They lay on the rocks and swam in the water.

The others all wanted to tan before they got to Tel Aviv in four days' time. Nathan didn't know why everyone wanted to tan, because they were already tanned. Mitch, a doctor, had for weeks before the trip taken a regimen of melanin injections, twice daily, straight into his belly, leaving his skin dark and bronze. Mitch still thought his skin could be more bronzed, more even.

He asked Nathan to take his photo and then he looked at the photo. He said, 'It's not quite right.'

Nathan lay back down on his stomach. Nathan flipped over. He applied more tanning oil. He draped a towel over his head, then rearranged the towel. He played with his chain. He listened to the sound of the water lapping against the rocks.

Dazed, Nathan got up and put on shorts, sneakers, then went for a walk. He walked along a trail on what was not really a mountain and not really a hill. It was windless and hot. He could hear cicadas and see the sea, a boat, a ferry, possibly the ferry, slowly crossing to the mainland or between one island and another. Nathan walked until he came to a wire fence. He stood there in front of the fence but couldn't pass it. Nathan felt something existential and diffuse, then, uneasy, went back to the rocks.

He sat down.

He said, 'We should really do something.'

———

In the morning, waking early and partially hungover, Nathan trekked into town alone, then took a bus to Palma.

In Palma, what Nathan did was stand in one square and then another. At an ATM he withdrew five hundred euros. He walked around the Old Town. He went into a Starbucks, then sat in the square outside the Starbucks drinking an iced coffee. His chair was on cobblestones. It wobbled. Nathan used the Starbucks's wifi and finished the iced coffee, then bought another. He felt caffeinated. On Grindr, he asked people where he could buy drugs. He asked this obliquely, with emojis. It was 10 a.m.

A man told him he had bought coke in the bar of a nearby hotel. Then the man wrote, 'I want you to fuck my face.'

Nathan walked to the hotel but the bar was closed.

Nathan defecated in the hotel bathroom, then walked through the hotel and descended a series of stairs onto the beach. It was the hotel's beach, the sand all white and powdery, the water clear. A man stood on a paddleboard and paddled. Small waves broke on the shore.

On the sand stood a line of hotel staff. They carried towels and looked like ageing tennis players, with tanned, creased skin and starched polos.

Nathan approached one of them. He was middle-aged. Nathan asked the beachboy if he knew where he could buy drugs.

The beachboy said, 'Twenty euro.'

Nathan gave him the money.

The beachboy walked up to a sun lounger. Nathan followed. The beachboy placed a towel on the lounger and said, 'Locker, five euro.'

Nathan shook his head. Nathan typed something into Google Translate and showed the beachboy. He squinted. Sunlight reflected off the screen. The beachboy nodded, then typed something into Nathan's phone in Spanish. Google translated: 'Go to the lobby.'

Nathan went and stood in the lobby, which was large and predominantly empty. Nathan was slightly on edge. It was possible, he thought, that the beachboy might report him, that the beachboy might betray him. Nathan watched people come in and out of the lobby. Nathan noticed a woman who was standing in the lobby wearing a backpack but wouldn't put the backpack down. Because Nathan looked at the woman, the woman looked at Nathan. He felt observed and overly exposed. He considered leaving the lobby.

A man tapped Nathan on the shoulder. It was a different beachboy. He looked like Rafael Nadal. Rafael Nadal motioned for Nathan to follow him. They walked outside and down the stairs to the beach. They stood on the landing between one flight and another. They both looked out at the water. It was like a second sun was in the water, like the water emitted its own light.

Rafael Nadal said, 'Two grams, two hundred.'

This seemed obscene. Nathan asked, 'Are you a cop?' because he'd read online that a cop had to tell you, though he didn't know if this applied in Spain. Rafael Nadal said, 'No.'

Nathan said okay, then handed him the notes. Rafael Nadal passed him a tiny bag and walked down the stairs.

Nathan went back into the hotel and into the bathroom. He entered a stall and locked the door.

In the toilet stall, Nathan was having a good time. He opened the tiny ziplock bag and did a key bump. Then he cut a line on his phone screen. He snorted it. He considered playing music. He put some music on with his earphones in, then snorted a little more.

He wanted to do coke at the villa, to have a drum track playing, for all of them to be dancing on the terrace.

There was a knock at the door.

Nathan paused the music. He waited.

There was another knock. The lock jiggled.

Nathan said, 'Occupato.'

Then there was a voice. It spoke Spanish.

Nathan said, 'Occupied.'

'Sir,' the voice said. 'I need to ask you to open the door.'

Nathan froze.

'We need you to come out of the stall now, sir.'

Nathan's heart beat rapidly. The voice sounded like a cop's. Nathan thought to ask the voice if they were a cop, then decided against it.

He looked at the bag. It would be bad if the bag was with him. If the bag was on his person. He looked for somewhere he could hide the bag. The toilet was the kind that didn't have a tank. He touched the wall looking for it.

'I'm not going to ask again. Please exit the stall.'

'Just a moment,' Nathan said. His hands shook. He thought this might be it. The bill was due. If he was arrested, Nathan thought, he would stay in the handcuffs, he wouldn't slip out. But he didn't want to be arrested.

He looked into the toilet bowl and opened the bag. He paused.

There was another knock. The voice said, 'Sir!' The door started to shake.

Nathan emptied the bag into the water. The coke clumped on the surface. Then he dropped the bag into the water. He went to flush the toilet but there was no button. He stepped back. The toilet flushed. The plastic bag whirled around the bowl, then floated. Nathan closed the lid.

He put his sunglasses on and opened the door.

It was the concierge and, behind him, a guest, the woman with the backpack.

'Sir,' the concierge said. 'This is the women's bathroom.'

Nathan felt multiple emotions in quick succession. Nathan said, 'Oh.'

Nathan nodded and left the bathroom. The concierge followed him. Nathan considered finding Rafael Nadal again but the concierge wouldn't leave him. He knew what was up. The concierge smiled and said, almost hissing, 'Sir, is there anything I can do for you?'

Nathan left the hotel.

He walked back to the station. Keeping his face expressionless, he passed vacationers, families, teenagers making their way to the beach, people at restaurants, their tables out on the street, laughing, vendors selling things that lit up and twirled and leapt into the air.

At the station, Nathan took the escalator down to the bus bays. He sat on a bench in front of a large metallic pillar and waited.

Through his sunglasses he looked at his reflection in the pillar, dark and distended. Nathan thought he must change his behaviour, that he must change his life. Then the thought left him, and he stared at his phone.

There were flecks of white on the screen, either coke or pocket lint. He licked his index finger. He pressed his finger on the flecks, then massaged them into his gums.

The person next to him on the bench got off the bench.

Back in town, Nathan bought two grams of coke, effortlessly and without suspense, at the bus stop. He went back to the house.

Jarred and Nathan stood in the smoking section on the club's rooftop in Tel Aviv. Nathan thought he recognised people he had seen over the past few days, sitting in the condo's pool or at a circuit party enclosed in chain-link fencing like a daytime pen on the beach, but he wasn't sure. Most of the bodies were naked or nearly naked.

At one point Nathan had been wearing an undershirt. He had taken the undershirt off and stuffed it down the waistband of his shorts. It was gone. Nathan was also wearing a dog collar he had bought online from a pet-supply store in Melbourne and packed in his luggage.

Two guys, also shirtless, both skinny, one in a harness, the other with a glow stick around his neck, asked Jarred if Jarred wanted to have sex with them. Jarred said no. They finished their cigarettes together and went downstairs. Jarred went into the dark room and had sex with them.

The dark room wasn't really its own room but a section of the main dance floor, partitioned off by a black curtain. Nathan stood next to the dark room but did not go into the dark room. The light in the club strobed.

Nathan went into the bathroom and did another line. He had bought ketamine mixed with what the dealer described as Berlin MDMA the day they had all arrived in Israel, at a Pride-branded pool party at a large family water park, while in line for the slide.

He came out of the bathroom.

Lasers sped across the ceiling, collapsed in on themselves and converged then shot back out. Nathan felt his perceptions were becoming clearer or that his thoughts were faster, like a higher-speed processor had been installed, all firewalls disabled, light elongating and streaking, his consciousness like time, something that could contract and expand. He chewed gum. He swayed.

Nathan noticed people smoking on the dance floor. Nathan lit a cigarette and smoked it. The ember reached the filter.

Nathan began to feel as though the same song had been playing for hours, that when the DJ would make a transition there was actually no transition, each track was the same track, each drop the same drop. Then the feeling left him, rapid and kinetic. Nathan danced a little. Nathan thought the word 'hectic'.

Nathan messaged other people from their Airbnb. Someone messaged back with the name of a club. Nathan went to the new club, but it wasn't the right club. He had misread the message. Nathan left the new club and went back to the first one.

On the street, the bouncer wouldn't let him in. The bouncer spoke in Hebrew and then English. The bouncer pointed at Nathan's wrist and said, 'Wristband.'

Nathan didn't know what he had done with his wristband. Nathan attempted to argue with the bouncer.

A group of men came out of the entrance. As the bouncer moved to let them pass, Nathan tried to dive in.

The bouncer grabbed Nathan's arm and twisted it, then pushed him back onto the street. Nathan said, 'We can be reasonable.'

The group of men laughed. They were large. They had muscles. They were American.

One of them said, 'What are you doing?'

Nathan didn't really know so he said, 'I don't know.'

They said they were going to a bar. One of them asked if Nathan wanted to come to the bar. Then one of them said, 'But you have to be our little bitch.'

Nathan hesitated. They were aggressive. Nathan couldn't tell if it was good aggressive or bad aggressive. There were four of them. This seemed novel.

He said, 'Sure.'

One of them said, 'I bet you're a little bitch that likes French movies.' Nathan didn't understand what the man was trying to say. Nathan replied, 'Yes.'

The group walked to McDonald's. Nathan was told to open the door. Nathan opened it. He held it open. Inside, they sat at a plastic table. They were on little stools. Nathan could feel the air-conditioning on his bare shoulders, his chest. There were phrases on the walls, some written in Hebrew and others in English. For a moment he thought he could read Hebrew but they were the words in English. He read the words 'Mega Big America' and, below that, 'Tempting'.

One of the Americans, Mega Big American, said, 'The little bitch buys the burgers.'

Nathan said he would not buy them burgers.

Another repeated, 'The bitch buys the burgers.'

A woman in a visor behind the ordering counter looked over at their table. Nathan could see her, behind Mega Big

American, in between a series of wooden slats. Nathan looked at his phone. His flight home was in forty-eight hours.

Nathan's body was very heavy. His skin was sunburnt and hot. Nathan had been rolling for three days. He thought about doing a line at the table, then remembered it was illegal to do a line at the table.

A Happy Meal was in front of him. Then the Happy Meal was taken away. 'The little bitch doesn't get any.' The men laughed.

Nathan repeated, 'I'm not buying your meals,' before realising they already had their meals. Nathan tried to be very still.

Mega Big American flicked a fry at Nathan, then said, 'The little bitch can have a single fry.'

The fry was on the ground. Nathan looked intently at the fry. Then the fry wasn't there. Nathan thought the fry had glitched, then realised it had been swept up by an employee.

The men were talking to him. Nathan wasn't really paying attention. His body felt like something distant and poorly remote-controlled. He stood up. Mega Big American asked where he was going. Nathan didn't say anything.

On the street there were still people. Nathan was on a main road. He recognised the twenty-four-hour grocery store, a falafel stand. Nathan walked until he was back at the Airbnb. He unlocked the door to the condo's foyer, went through to the courtyard, and began climbing the building's stairs.

At the landing, his key didn't work. The door wouldn't open.

Nathan sat on the landing and leant against the apartment door. The door was not in fact his apartment door but the door to the apartment beneath his.

Nathan sat there. He heard the whine of a passing scooter, then a car with its windows down, bass rippling the air. Nathan closed his eyes.

He saw phosphenes. Sparks. A burning filament. A bright light.

In Bright Light

The court awarded damages. The damages were more than two-point-nine million dollars. The sum was for current and future lost earnings, to be paid by a media conglomerate that had published certain allegations. They were not Alice's lost earnings, they were a man's, but for one long afternoon her name, among others, trended on Twitter, and for weeks afterwards Alice's phone vibrated with phone calls and emails and text messages. Alice changed her number. Then people found the new number. They called her family. They called people she had gone to school with, other actors, crew members on films she had starred in.

For a while Alice had thought she still might be sued. There were conference calls linking one side of the Pacific to the other. Legal counsel in Australia, the States. She took the calls on her patio where her cell didn't cut out. Risk was discussed. Then it looked like she wouldn't be sued as long as she didn't make another statement. But people wanted her to make a statement. Then they tired. The news cycle moved on.

As it happened, Alice rarely left the house, a small, two-bedroom mid-century she owned in Los Feliz, all dark wood, hillside views and glass. She wasn't working. She took in a shelter dog, a black greyhound named Brando. Brando had a scrunched-up face like a boxer's. He had suffered. Brando ran around the house and peed on the floorboards, the tiles, Alice's bed. His black lips parted, his tongue lolling out. To put his leash on, they wrestled. He bared his teeth. At night Brando looked like a demon, a jackal. After four days Alice took the greyhound back. She apologised to the shelter staff, and in the hope they would not speak to reporters, donated a sum of money. The shelter staff spoke to reporters.

Alice's friend, an actress who had become an executive producer for a successful show on a streaming service, had an assistant deliver Alice a clear quartz stone. It came in a box and inside the box was a handwritten note. Alice couldn't tell if her friend had written the note or if the assistant had. The note told her the stone could magnify intentions, and just as you could see through the stone to what was behind and in front of it, it would allow you to look through the present and see the same.

Alice didn't do what the note told her to do. She didn't meditate with the stone, but she did sometimes, when anxious, eat an edible, one or a handful of gummies, and hold the quartz as she lay in bed or on top of her bed, and though she didn't think her intentions magnified or gained a sense of clarity, she felt something. Like the glass of an air-conditioned room, the stone was cool to touch, and Alice sensed that outside, Los Angeles stretched beyond her windows like an establishing shot, across and over the sycamores and palms, the stucco houses, the lanes of traffic and canyons and valleys, the forty-five-foot letters in sheet metal and below them the private pools that littered the hills, little dappled points of light.

The hard thing, as Alice saw it, was that something bad had happened to her, and it was private and then it wasn't. Now when people thought of her, Alice intuited, they didn't really think of her. They thought about someone else and the things that someone did. Or that she was manipulative, opportunistic, untruthful, a whore. The people who thought these things also said them, online.

The actual event in her mind had long since taken on a kind of filmic shorthand. A meeting in a hotel room, a room of people emptying to two, the declined offer of a drink, an embroidered robe coming undone. A jump cut. Then Alice, alone in a carpeted hallway, stepping aside for housekeeping to pass.

This had happened a long time ago, after Alice had appeared in a string of independent features, cheap mumble-core dramas, but before she had been to Cannes, before her fame had waxed and begun to wane, and before she'd starred in the studio-backed period piece which was both critically and commercially a failure but allowed Alice to purchase her house outright.

A decade had passed and Alice had continued acting. Then the exposé came out and her name was mentioned among others', and Alice didn't know how her name came to be mentioned, or whether she should say something or not say something, each choice having the potential to be damaging but damaging in different ways. She made a public statement, then she regretted making the public statement, then she regretted regretting the statement.

Alice was in a period between jobs, a period she was intimately familiar with, when it could seem like she might never work again, and then something would come up and she'd be out on location, submerged in bright light, surrounded by technicians or the thin walls of an RV trailer, colour-coded Post-it-noted scripts spread out before her.

But a role didn't come.

Alice understood that she needed to do something, but what that something was seemed unclear to her, difficult to articulate. Standing on her patio, Alice called her agent, Brett. But Brett didn't answer. It was his assistant. Then Alice realised it wasn't his assistant but someone else. Alice said, 'Put me through to Brett,' then the voice said, 'Okay,' and then Alice was on hold and then she was taken off hold, and she could hear something, a voice, Brett's but muffled. Then she was back on hold. Then the first person answered and said, 'Brett's in a meeting,' so Alice said, 'Who am I speaking to?' and the voice said, 'I'm the intern.' Alice said, 'I'll leave a message,' but it was too late. The line was dead.

Alice began to take small trips out of the house. Instead of calling out her myotherapist, she got into her car and drove to her myotherapist's office suite. She lay on a white towel and listened to the gurgle of a water diffuser. She was touched and had delicate acupuncture needles placed into her shoulders and neck. She ordered and drank iced coffees sitting at roadside tables. Sometimes Alice noticed a black van idling and her pulse would quicken, and then the van would keep going and she'd realise it was following someone else, a realisation that sometimes made her feel better and sometimes made her feel worse.

She wandered through luxury department stores. She went to Nordstrom. She ran her hand across bedding as a sales attendant described thread counts. She couldn't tell if the attendant recognised her or not.

Alice asked, 'Does it come in a set?'

She took the set home, washed the sheets then let them dry in the sun. It was late in the afternoon. She ate a gummy, not because she was anxious but for the feeling of everything becoming soft around the edges. Then Alice lay on the living-room carpet and watched the light turn technicolour, then fail.

Her mother called from Melbourne. Alice's mother described the things she had to do or things that had happened to Alice's sister, her nieces, the trip her sister was planning, how she'd bought her children travelling clothes, filled out passport forms, visas. And though the call often cut in and out, Alice repeated, 'That's nice. That's nice.'

Alice still spoke with her mother, though they didn't really talk; their lives had diverged so much that they no longer shared a frame of reference.

When Alice had only been in LA one year her parents had flown to visit her. They had visited her apartment, at the time a walk-up off Fountain Avenue Alice rented with three other women. All actresses.

Alice's mother had entered all of the bedrooms and taken the curtains off their rails. She'd asked Alice where the washing machine was. Alice said that she didn't have a washing machine, that she went to a laundromat. Alice's mum held the curtains and frowned.

Her father pointed outside the window and asked, 'Is that a coyote?' Alice's apartment looked down onto the complex's trash cans.

Alice said, 'No, that's just someone's dog.'

Alice's parents didn't want Alice to stay in her apartment while they were there but with them in their hotel. It had a pool. Her father said he would sleep on the floor. Alice said no.

Alice took her parents to Hollywood Boulevard to walk the Walk of Fame. She wore large sunglasses. Her parents walked on the stars, the scuffed terrazzo, and read the names aloud. Her father said, 'One day you'll have one,' and Alice said nothing but felt something keenly, something close to pain, because though it was tacky he had said exactly what it was she wanted.

On the corner of Hollywood and Vine a woman lay in the centre of the intersection. She was yelling. She screamed. She had her arms above her head and rolled. Cars slowed, honked. They drove around her then away. Alice's parents wanted to help. They began walking onto the road. Alice adjusted her sunglasses. People honked at her parents. It took a moment for Alice to realise she was still only watching.

'Are you listening?' Alice's mother's voice now leaked out of the phone.

Alice slept and didn't dream.

_____

'We're only doing the set cocktails.'

Alice said she didn't drink. Alice felt she was already a little high.

'Like I said, it's set.'

Alice thought he was probably an actor. Pouring drinks, he was like everyone else. Playing a role.

'Just give me a Diet Coke,' she said.

The Diet Coke came with a slice of lemon floating in the glass. She took the lemon out with her fingers and walked out onto the deck. She dropped the slice in a garden bed, brought the glass to her lips. She felt light, like air.

Alice wasn't sure whose house it was. She rarely went to parties in LA anymore but had decided to come to this one, coaxed by her friend Frances. Frances was twenty-two, had acted professionally the same number of years Alice had—since she was six—and took college credits online. They had filmed a movie together, years ago, in Vancouver, going to the same bad karaoke bar after shoots, and still kept in touch. To Alice, the Hollywood Frances inhabited seemed more exciting than the one she did.

The party was in a large house cut into the Brentwood hillside. The house was like being in the future: sleek glass, polished concrete floors. There was a pool and people by the pool but not yet in the pool. Alice stood next to it. She knew Frances wasn't there.

Across the pool Alice could see an actress who was more famous than she was, someone who could be recognised by first name. People were crowding her. They looked where she looked while never quite looking away from her.

They waited to see where her attention was, to talk about what she wanted to talk about. Alice had spent so much time in LA, more than a decade, almost two, but this was still something she found difficult to tell, whether the actress was innately magnetic or if it was just the fame, so much fame that you could see it like a bend in the surrounding light.

Alice looked away. Whenever Alice was at a party with a pool she remembered an industry party she'd gone to when she first came here. She'd been twenty-three. The party had been hosted by an Australian funding body. There were agents and casting directors all at a hotel, a rooftop bar in the city. There was a pool. A girl, an actress, decided to jump in the pool because she thought it would be funny or that it would show that she was fun, that she could be magnetic. But no one else got in the pool and the girl waited and then got out of the pool and the bar staff gave her a t-shirt and the t-shirt was branded with the name of the hotel. The woman went to the bathroom and then came back, and stood on the rooftop, still damp, wearing the branded t-shirt over her dress. And she'd stood there, Alice watching, with an expression that was still smiling but also fake, and the girl stayed like that for a while and then she left.

Alice felt like the girl standing wet by the pool, though she was dry and at a different pool and would not go in. She kept thinking people were looking at her, kept seeing faces in her peripheral vision, but when she turned her head no one was looking.

Someone said, 'Alice.' A woman was moving towards her. She was a short, middle-aged woman, dressed like a receptionist. She said, 'Frances isn't here yet.' Then she apologised.

'Sorry, I'm Terri. I'm Frances's manager.' Alice looked at her. 'Sometimes we go out together,' Terri said. 'It isn't weird.'

Alice and Terri stood next to each other. Terri looked across the pool and saw the famous woman.

Terri said, 'Is that Kirsten?'

Alice said, 'Yes.'

Terri looked like she wanted to go over. She didn't. She told Alice that Frances had shot a fragrance campaign earlier that day. Alice didn't know when Frances had become famous enough to head a fragrance campaign. Terri said Frances was planning on having a big night. Terri said she had twins, four-year-olds, but tonight there was a sitter so she would also have a big night. Terri repeated 'big night'. Then Terri toasted the sitter. She struck her glass against Alice's but Alice didn't expect it and dropped her glass.

It didn't break. Alice picked up the now-empty glass. Some people were looking at her.

Terri waved at someone for another drink, then she narrowed her eyes at Alice. 'We should do a meeting sometime.' Then she said, 'Who's your manager?'

Alice said she didn't have one. Then Terri asked who her agent was. Alice told her.

'Oh, I don't like Brett,' Terri said. 'No one likes Brett. He isn't classy.'

Alice said, 'Brett's okay.'

'We were on the same flight once,' Terri said. 'Brett and I. This was coming back from Cannes. He was in first so I had to walk past him and he was wearing sunglasses and this cap, this A24 baseball cap. The logo embroidered. You get me. He was wearing an embroidered baseball cap and drinking champagne, and when I went past him he gave me this stupid smile. He's an idiot. Fuck him and that cap.'

Alice stood quietly.

'He does TM.' Alice already knew this. Brett did transcendental meditation. He had spent a large amount of money in an office suite off Santa Monica Boulevard, was given a mantra and often recommended Alice do the same.

Alice was still quiet.

'I mean,' Terri said, 'he's a fine agent.'

Alice made her way to one of the bathrooms. She felt unsteady. It seemed very important to get to the bathroom. Inside, Alice locked the door then climbed into the bathtub. It was the kind that had been sculpted from a single piece of stone. It was cool on her skin. Alice took out her phone and opened Frances's Instagram.

She watched her latest story. Frances was with a group of people in cowboy hats. Alice didn't know why they were wearing cowboy hats. Alice decided to call Frances. Frances didn't answer so Alice called again. She answered. She said she was close. Alice heard giggling. She heard a man's voice. Alice asked where Frances was. 'I'm still at home. But I'm close. I'm on my way.' Someone giggled again.

Alice got off the phone. She stayed in the bathtub for a while. Occasionally, someone beat their hand against the door. Then she looked at Instagram again. There was a new story. Frances was in a different cowboy hat. Frances held a toy gun.

Alice decided to leave the party. She called a Lyft. But there was a gate and the Lyft wouldn't have the code for the gate, so when Alice left the party she walked down the driveway, went through the gate, then a second gate she didn't remember passing on the way in. She stood on the road and waited for the car. At times she thought she saw faces in the dark.

The Lyft was air-conditioned. In the cabin, the air was sweet and cool. The driver asked whose house she'd been at, what was the party. Alice said she wasn't sure, then put earphones in. She didn't put music on. The car drove.

He didn't take the 405. The car wound through the Hills. It was very dark. The road curved. They passed gated drive after gated drive. Every now and then the trees would open and Alice could see the lights of the city below. They were driving for a long time. Alice slowly began to feel that they were driving in the wrong direction, that they weren't approaching her house but moving somewhere else. The driver speeding out of LA, taking her to the desert, somewhere desolate and vast. She imagined terrible and perverse things. She looked at her phone. She couldn't track the ride's route because, like in so many parts of the Hills, she'd lost signal. She panicked. She put a hand on the door. She wanted to test whether it was locked. She thought she would just open it. A test. She looked in the rear-view mirror and saw the driver's eyes. They met hers. Alice gasped.

The driver pulled over. Alice was home.

In bed, Alice thought she shouldn't take so many edibles. Alice thought she needed to leave LA.

Her sister invited her on their trip. Her sister and nieces were going to New York. It was her nieces' first time leaving

Australia. Alice understood that the invitation was a gesture. Alice and her sister rarely spoke. She said yes.

First her sister and nieces would fly from Melbourne to LAX, where Alice would join them, and from there they would board a domestic flight together. Alice would stay with them for the week—she had impulsively upgraded their accommodation to a two-bedroom suite at the Plaza—then return home while they flew on to Disney World, Orlando.

Alice's sister made an itinerary and emailed it to Alice three weeks before they stepped on a plane.

There was news. The week before the trip Brett contacted her. She'd been approached for a role.

She met the directors that week, two brothers who worked together, as well as their casting director, in a wood-panelled office in West Hollywood. Her agent had described them as exciting. They wore basketball shoes and were younger than Alice. They hadn't sent her a whole script, only a scene. The scene was a woman confessing that something horrible had been done to her. Alice wasn't sure if it was the kind of role she wanted, or, if she took it, what exactly it would mean.

The brothers said they had written the role with someone like her in mind. 'The money people want someone hot right now, but that isn't what it should be. Fuck the money people.' They listed a few other actresses. Alice recognised them. They were actresses who had been written about in exposés. They wanted to test Alice because they were fans of her early work. 'It felt real,' one of the brothers told her, 'like you were close to something.'

'We want that for the role,' the other said. 'She's complicated.'

Alice did what she always did with directors: she repeated them. She said, 'Complicated.'

'Exactly,' the other said.

'What we want to know is whether you can do something. If you can take us to that spot. We don't want you to give us everything, but we want to feel everything.'

'We want next level. Something more interesting than what you've done before.'

Alice thought the performances she had done before were interesting. Alice replied, 'Next level.' Then she did the test, the casting director holding a camcorder, one of the brothers recording with his phone.

She felt what she always felt acting, even in a test. She felt the relief of being someone else.

For the next few days she didn't hear anything. Then there was a call-back, and another call-back. One brother called her incredible. The other told her she had what they wanted. She asked her agent, 'Do I need to test again?' Brett said, 'Definitely not.' She had the part. Alice asked whether he was telling her she had the part or the directors had said she had the part. Brett replied, 'These are details.'

Alice went to the airport. She passed security. She remembered there were edibles in her bag. She didn't know whether or not she could have edibles in her bag. She took them out and dropped them in a clear plastic bin. She did this discreetly, then she waited.

Her nieces were excited to see her but they were also tired. Her nieces were thirteen and eight years old. When they saw her at their gate they yelled, 'Auntie Alice!' Alice mainly saw her nieces in Skype calls. In person was different. Like a very small dog, her younger niece had too much energy in too small a container.

As they were boarding their flight, the attendant looked at her passport and then said Alice's full name. Some people looked at her. Alice took her passport and walked onto the plane.

Alice's nieces wanted Alice to sit next to them so she sat between them. Alice's sister took a Valium and a strong antihistamine chased with another Valium. She lowered her eye mask. She slept.

Alice's younger niece, Emily, said she wanted to watch *Cars*. Alice searched the in-flight entertainment system. They didn't have *Cars*.

Alice's older niece, Claudia, said they had to watch something else, and Emily whined. She put her hands in the air and sort of flailed them. She made a noise. A person in front of them turned in their seat.

Alice said, 'Both of you shut your eyes,' then slid two Hershey's bars out of her bag. She told them to open their eyes. She gave them the Hershey's bars. Emily was excited by American candy. She hugged her. Claudia left hers on her tray table.

They watched a film in which computer-generated fish danced underwater. It finished so they began another. When she felt Emily get restless, Alice opened her bag and handed her another chocolate bar.

Claudia didn't watch the film but asked about famous people Alice had been in movies with. Then she said names of celebrities and asked if Alice knew them. And Alice said, 'No, no, no, yes,' and Claudia said, 'That's so cool.'

Then Claudia asked if she could take a selfie of them together and Alice said okay. Claudia looked at the photo for a long time and then said it was good.

Emily fell asleep, her breath soft like a small animal's, a trail of chocolate dribbling down her chin. The lights of the cabin dimmed. Claudia put a hand on Alice's shoulder and looked up at her. She said, 'I believe you.' It took a moment for Alice to realise what it was Claudia believed. Alice didn't know what to say so she said, 'Cool.'

When Alice got off the flight she had four missed calls. They were from her agent.

'Okay, they need you to test again,' Brett said. 'They want you, but they want you to test blonde. They need you today or tomorrow.'

Alice didn't make it to the hotel. She took a flight back.

In LA she wore a bad wig then a worse wig then resorted to a Vons-bought packet dye. The test was delayed one day, then another. The ends of her hair split, frayed. To calm herself she drove to a dispensary. She stocked up: sativa, indica, hybrids. She drove back home.

Her sister called from the Plaza. Since having children, whenever she was mad Alice's sister spoke in a whisper. She whispered, then she whispered some more. Alice did what she always did when her family was mad at her: she sent a hamper. Because her sister was in New York she chose Sahadi's. She rang the store. She wanted to substitute the candied figs. The attendant said eight-year-olds would eat candied figs. Alice said okay and bought the basket.

Alice did the test. She didn't get the part.

———

Sometimes Alice thought that if she looked deep inside of herself, she'd find an animal, something coiled, something snarling. Alone in bed she looked for it and found nothing there.

Alice lay on the living-room carpet and emailed her agent. In the months since the test Brett had stopped taking her calls. The actor involved in her case had had a film released. A small group of women picketed the premiere. Other than that, no one mentioned it. Alice wrote that she wanted a meeting. The sound of a helicopter, somewhere over the hills, passed, the glass of the house softly shaking. Then Alice wrote a more assertive email. She lay there. Outside, the city was like a piece of impure quartz, everything diffuse, covered in haze. Alice refreshed her emails.

Her niece Claudia had emailed to say that she understood why Alice had had to leave them. The email also shared an article from *Teen Vogue* about a certain actress. Claudia didn't think it was right that people thought the actress was crazy but she agreed with *Teen Vogue* that the situation the actress was in was crazy, the system. *Teen Vogue* wrote that you could change the system. Since the flight, Claudia often sent Alice emails. Other times she emailed articles that quoted different actresses' Twitter accounts, their tweets and the tweets other celebrities or annoying people on the internet tweeted in response. The conversation. Or Claudia would email that one of her friends had seen a movie Alice was in and what the friend had thought. Claudia had turned fourteen.

Alice thought the articles were stupid. She didn't read them but wrote back things like, 'Wow,' or 'I'll have to read it later,' and then her niece would ask about when she thought it would be okay for her to come to LA and stay with her. To that, Alice didn't reply.

Alice watched television. She rented a film people tweeted about in relation to *Teen Vogue* articles. The movie was about sexual harassment in broadcast news. Alice rented it off Amazon for $14.99. She began to watch it. In the film a famous actress plays a news anchor, wears prosthetics and speaks in a slightly lower voice. The voice doesn't really have inflections, it's just lower. The performance was nominated for an Academy Award. Watching it, Alice said a few things in a lowered voice. She read her emails to Brett aloud. Alice said, 'I want to have a meeting.' Alice said, 'This is unacceptable.' Alice said, 'My schedule is free.'

She laughed. She was alone in her house. Alice turned off the film.

The reporter sat in Alice's living room. Alice poured mineral water then put the glasses on coasters. Alice had to concentrate on giving even pours. This was tricky.

She had spent the early afternoon changing from one outfit to another, sometimes swallowing gummies whole. She'd only wanted to take a little, hoping to balance one with the other, one making her go down and the other up. Then she'd taken some more, recalibrated, and then later, seated in the living room wearing Rag & Bone jeans, thinking, Rag & Bone jeans, she took a little more.

The reporter was Terri's idea. Terri, Frances's manager, had taken Alice on as a new client, fired Brett, and had a plan for what Alice had to do. Terri had a specific vision. At no point would Alice discuss specific allegations. That was the past.

'I'm excited we're doing this,' the reporter said. The reporter was a woman in black jeans and a sweater. She didn't do *Vanity Fair* profiles or *Harper's Bazaar*—she wrote for *The New York Times*. Alice didn't think producers or casting agents read *The New York Times*.

Alice went to say, 'Me too,' but stopped herself at 'Me.'

There was a knock at the door. Alice opened it. Two men came inside carrying camera equipment and lights. Alice asked what was happening. 'I was told the photographer was Wednesday.'

'Oh, it's not a big deal. He'll take the photos while we talk. It'll be simple. Laid-back.'

The photographer walked up to different walls, looked at them. The photographer asked if they could look at the patio. Alice nodded very slowly but they hadn't waited. They were already outside, then they came back inside. They seemed to move both overly slow and too fast for Alice to follow.

The reporter picked up a book on the coffee table. The reporter asked, 'Is this what you're reading or what you put out for the profile?'

Alice said, 'Sorry?'

'I'm joking.'

'Oh, okay.' Alice wasn't really listening. Alice was trying not to seem high.

'I want to start on something simple,' the reporter said. The reporter began speaking about a court case, a case that hadn't directly involved Alice, but suggested things about a shift in culture. Alice heard the words 'shift in culture'. She wasn't sure what the question was.

'Excuse me,' Alice said. 'I just need a minute.' She got up and walked to the bathroom and shut the door.

She went through the things Terri had told her. 'We'll say you're waiting for the right role but that it needs to be cerebral. Complex. You're reading scripts. You're not just playing anyone. You want something real. You're still waiting for the new Hollywood. The one to come.'

Alice mouthed the words. Her hands felt hot so she washed them. She looked at her hands, then she looked at her reflection. She noticed something had happened to her vision. It was like she had been watching a 2D movie that was now 3D.

This seemed funny.

Alice did not want to do the interview, any interview. She didn't want to speak about certain things or represent them on-screen, but this was the situation she was in. A situation where the things she wouldn't do became mixed with the things she did. So Alice decided to do something else.

She opened the bathroom window. She let out a laugh. She stopped herself, then she opened her mouth and laughed quietly. She put a foot up to the window, then an arm. She climbed out. And when she was standing on the patio she didn't stop. With her bare hands and feet, at the house's lowest point, she pulled herself onto the roof.

She sat down. What she could see was like the view from her living room except for the expanse of the sky.

It was sunset, the sky a blaze of orange and pink. She thought about the reporter and the photographer and his assistant in her living room. She thought about them sitting in the fading light, sitting there until the room went dark. At some point they would leave. She thought, I'll wait them out. She giggled. Alice thought she couldn't sit on the roof forever but that she could sit there for a long time. She would do transcendental meditation. She'd see it all and transcend it. She looked out. She could see past the eucalyptus trees of her yard, the cacti, and out past the palms, the entire city.

She said, 'I fucking hate this place.' She laughed. Then she said it again and again.

Acknowledgements

Thank you to Stephen Kilpatrick, Kent D. Wolf, Caspian Dennis, Jane Palfreyman and Hannah Westland.

Thank you to the editors and journals who have worked on and published these stories in slightly differing forms. The team at *Granta*, especially Josie Mitchell, Luke Neima and Eleanor Chandler, Emily Stokes at *The Paris Review*, Tess Smurthwaite at *Meanjin*, Halimah Marcus at *Electric Literature*, Jordan Castro at *New York Tyrant* and Patrick Cottrell and the team at *McSweeney's*. I also thank the team at Allen & Unwin, including Tom Bailey-Smith, Sam Cooney and Clara Finlay.

Thank you to my friends and readers Emma Marie Jones, Lauren Lauterhahn, my writing mentor Abigail Ulman, Matthew Dalla Rosa, Laura Stortenbeker, Oliver Reeson, Oliver Mol, Becca Schuh, Bella Johansson, Samuel Rutter, Nathan Smith and Georgia Delaney. Thank you as well to my family.

I am indebted to Chelsea Hodson and the late Giancarlo DiTrapano who have in one way or another taught me how to better write or live.

Part of the book was written while I was undertaking a PhD at RMIT University and I thank my supervisors Ronnie Scott and Julienne van Loon. I am thankful for other funding I received while writing the book, including the University of Melbourne's Felix Meyer Scholarship, the Wheeler Centre Hot Desk Fellowship and the Next Wave Writer-in-Residence.